Terror in the Night

A Product of Evil in our Society

Michael J

authorHOUSE®

AuthorHouse™
1663 Liberty Drive
Bloomington, IN 47403
www.authorhouse.com
Phone: 1 (800) 839-8640

Published by AuthorHouse   08/06/2015

ISBN: 978-1-5049-2190-9 (sc)
ISBN: 978-1-5049-2189-3 (e)

Library of Congress Control Number: 2015910945

Print information available on the last page.

PREFACE

My personal convictions have lead me to write this book. Even though it is a work of fiction you will likely see some truth as you read. I don't pretend to have all of the answers, I don't even pretend to have <u>any</u> answers, regarding why violence exists to the extent that it does. I am a Christian and I believe that the 'Fall of Man' has a great deal to do with the problem. I also believe that while there is some good in every (well almost every) person I believe that everyone has a sinful nature. Many of us have been able, through various means, to overcome the desire to act upon the negative sort of feelings that we all have. The problem is that <u>far too many</u> people, again for various reasons, have not been able to overcome the desire to do harm to their fellow human beings.

I'm not an expert in human behavior. I'm just an <u>observer</u> of human behavior. Like many others, I don't like what I have observed (seen). I have, however, learned that even though I don't like what I see going on around me, there isn't much I can do to have any real impact on the situation.

So, what <u>can</u> I do? Not much really. But then again, I can write about it. Why not do an expose' on all of the acts of violence going on in my own city?

Well, as you can see, I chose to write this book. Will this book change anything? Perhaps. I only know that I will feel a lot better about myself knowing that I have at least made some attempt to increase the awareness of the problem.

Enjoy!

****

Terror in the night,

Children take to flight.

Fear becomes a living thing.

Security shatters along with dreams.

Afraid to leave, not wanting to stay,

Realizing too late they must get away.

****

This poem is dedicated to the many children caught in domestic violence. They are too young and/or too afraid to escape so they face daily abuse of one kind or another.

PART ONE

Terror Rears its Ugly Head

CHAPTER ONE

The City

It was just after midnight when the call came into the station. A body had been found just outside of the coliseum. The area was not particularly known to be where a crime would occur, certainly not murder. The two homicide detectives who were assigned to the case were Jack Carlson and his partner of over ten years, Maggie Donaldson. They arrived at the scene where several police and the media had already gathered. There was also a rather large crowd of curious on-lookers. With the police cruisers (marked cars with flashing lights), the detectives' cars (unmarked but still with flashing lights) it looked like a major crime scene. Add to all of this the number of on-lookers, both in cars and on foot, it was quite crowded. It became a major task for the two homicide detectives to make their way to the body. "What were all these people doing out on the street at this hour?"

North Bend is basically like any other mid-western city. It is home to just over 400,000 people. Over the years the city has undergone changes not unlike other parts of the U.S. Businesses open while others close. North Bend was, at one time, a major hub of the steel industry. Today, most of the ground upon which huge mills and factories stood, now is home to sub-divisions, strip-malls and a few small businesses. It gets really warm in the summer and very cold in the winter. Some say there are only two seasons in North Bend – winter and summer. It's typical for winter to hang on until late March or early April. Then, with very little warning, it's suddenly warm and it rains almost every day until August. Then things dry up, it gets warmer but the evenings seem cooler with each passing day. I've cut my grass as late as Thanksgiving week-end and I've witnessed the first snowfall just before Halloween. I wouldn't be surprised if you (the reader) has something similar to say about the city where you live. Anytime the conversation becomes dull or awkward all you have to do is mention the weather. Am I right? That subject will usually supply you enough 'stuff' to talk about for a long time.

This has been my home since I was three years old. My parents grew tired of the 'big city' and decided to move just slightly more than a hundred miles away from Chicago. I don't remember much about living in Chicago but I'm a frequent visitor to the 'windy city'. I still have relatives there. As far back as I can remember I've been a fan of the Chicago Cubs. I think that may be due, in part, to the fact that my Dad loved the White Sox. He and I rarely agreed on anything.

As far as the crime rate goes, North Bend doesn't even come close to that of Chicago. We still have our share. Mostly burglary, robbery, assault and some gang violence. However, in my opinion, there is far too much domestic violence. I haven't compared North Bend to other cities of similar size but it seems to me that the per capita rate is higher here. In my opinion, numbers, comparisons and all of that doesn't matter so much as the fact that violence, especially domestic violence, occurs at all. The fact that it even exists is unacceptable and it needs to be addressed.

The detectives arrived at the crime scene - "What do we have?" Jack asked the uniformed officer. "Looks like the guy's been here for just a few hours. I'd say he's been beaten to death." "What makes you say that?" Maggie inquired. "Well, I don't see no stab wounds. And there ain't no sign of any bullet wounds. It doesn't even look like he put up much of a fight either," was the officer's reply.

The M.E. (medical examiner) arrived. After both Maggie and Jack made a search for ID in the victim's pockets and carefully examined the bruises and abrasions on the victim's body he was taken to the city morgue to determine the cause of death, approximate age, etc. They would also take prints from the victim. This information along with DNA might help them to make a positive ID on the victim.

The autopsy revealed the cause of death was due to blunt force trauma. He had, indeed, been beaten to death. But with what? And why? Who was this guy and how did he get here? The M.E.'s report revealed a fractured skull, several broken ribs, both arms broken, one leg shattered. There were ligature marks on his wrists and ankles indicating that he had been bound. This could be the reason for the absence of signs of a struggle. His fingertips were burned (probably acid) and it made it difficult to get decent prints. The coroner, "he probably died of shock after being tied up. I would guess that the burns on his fingers were done post-mortem. At least he was spared the pain of having all ten finger tips burned to a crisp."

Detective Carlson "Where do we start? Well, first we need to ID the guy and then we'll go from there." Where is 'there' and what will they do when they get there? They continue the investigation.

Just a week later two more bodies were found. One male and one female. The M.O. seemed to be somewhat different. No ID but this time they were able to obtain fingerprints. The location was about 10 miles east of the city in what would eventually be the basement of a new house. The builders had only completed the footings and foundation. No walls, no framing. Just a hole in the ground.

A break came in the first case when they matched the DNA from the victim with a felon who had a rather lengthy rap sheet. Now, they needed to determine his address.

In the second case, they were able to lift one print from one finger of the female victim. Now they were making some progress.

The first victim's name was Albert Millar. He had been released from prison after serving 6 years of a ten year sentence for assault (his girlfriend), public intoxication, assaulting an officer and raping his girlfriend's 13 year old daughter. The rape charges were later dropped. It seems like her mother had a little chat with her 13 year old and the sex was consensual. She (the child) had made a mistake. She wanted Albert to 'do her'. The charge was reduced from rape to statutory rape. This resulted in 'the son-of-a-bitch' serving far less time than he deserved. The girl's mother turned up dead a short time later. Even though Albert was on the streets, (he had somehow managed to make bail on a $500,000 bond) he alibied out for the time of the murder but they could never find enough to nail the bastard. The case is still open but the people working the case refuse to let it go cold. They feel like if they keep working the case something or someone will be found that will prove he killed her. But now, with Albert dead......

He had been out of prison for just under two years. He was living with a woman who he met just two months following his release from prison.

5

She has four children ages 8 through 15. Two girls and two boys. She had called the police on him several times. The police calls were primarily for assault on the girlfriend. The police arrested him several times. But she always refused to file charges. According to her, he's a good guy. She loves him very much and so do her kids.

Thanks to the many police calls, the detectives knew where to find Albert's 'family.' She and the kids were brought to the station for questioning. The police were curious to see what she knew about the assault on Albert. Did she know if he had enemies? Was he doing drugs? Was her boyfriend involved in any illicit activities? How well did she really know Albert?

The 'interview' had barely gotten started when she sprang to her feet and leaned on the table looking nose to nose with Jack. "What did he do? Whatever he did, I wasn't involved. I ain't seen him for several days. Am I under arrest?" She was not very happy about being pulled out of her home and taken to the station. The cops didn't understand that she had 'things' to do. The way she was shaking whatever drug she was on was starting to wear off.

In the interrogation room at the police station both detectives had been questioning Allicia (Albert's girlfriend and mother of the four kids). She stood by her story that Al was a great guy and they had never had any major problems. The officers that escorted her said that as far as they knew, Albert hadn't committed a crime. He had been involved in what appeared to be a fight.

Detective Carlson was beginning to lose patience with the restless, nervous Allicia. "Look lady, I've had about all I can take of you and the way you seem to be protecting your late boyfriend. I think it's time to have a little chat with your children. We'll see what they have to say about Albert." Allicia was startled, "no, wait, I thought Albert had just been beaten up. You didn't tell me he was dead. Please, just leave the kids alone. They all got along great with Albert." Allicia was left in interrogation room number one to cool off.

The detectives separated the kids thinking it best to interview them individually. They didn't want to take the risk of having one of them intimidating or influencing any of the others. This turned out to be a very good idea. One which produced results beyond what they expected. At the risk of frightening them or making them uneasy, they thought it best if both detectives conducted the interviews together. They started with the oldest. The 15 year old Sabrina.

The moment that Detective Carlson asked the 15 year old Sabrina if she liked her Mom's late boyfriend Albert, the girl began to cry, almost scream. She then started shaking as though she was freezing to death. She hadn't yet been told that Albert was dead.

"What's wrong honey? You can tell me. I promise nobody is going to be mad at you or hurt you." Maggie was trying to win the young girl's confidence.

Even though it isn't always appropriate, Maggie took the shaking, sobbing Sabrina into her arms. Tears began to flow down Maggie's cheeks as well. She knew that this child had been through some very difficult, horrifying experiences. Maggie had been abused herself when she was just about Sabrina's age. The 'story' began to unfold as Sabrina talked about what she had endured over the past twenty months. She referred to Albert as a 'monster'. She told about how he would enter her room at night. With her little sister in the bed next to hers. The 'monster' would get under the covers with her. Most of the time he was naked. He would undress her and …..

She couldn't go any further right now. The detectives really didn't want to hear much more either. At least not at the moment.

Neither of the boys said anything about sexual assault by Albert but both indicated that he had beaten them on several occasions. Mostly for small things like breaking something or spilling something. Henry (the ten year old) told the detectives that there was this one time when Albert beat him so hard that he couldn't go to school for several days. He said "my Mom didn't want people asking no questions about the cuts and bruises and my two missing teeth."

"Why do you think Albert beat you so bad that time? Did anyone take you to the doctor or emergency room?" "Mom said we can't afford no doctor or hospital. So she just put some medicine on me and a wet rag on my head and arms. Albert got really mad at me cause I went into Sabrina's room to ask her something. I thought she was just in there reading or something like that. Well, she wasn't reading nothing. He was in there with her, on top of her. She was crying. She didn't have no clothes on either.

Albert got off of her and hit me with the back of his hand and told me to get outta there and go to my room. I went to my room and I heard him yelling and hittin' Sabrina. Then Sabrina started screamin' and he hit her again. She stopped screamin' after that. Then I could hear him comin' toward my room. I got so scared I peed my pants. He came in and next thing I know he was hittin' and kickin' me. It hurt so bad I just fell asleep.

When I woke up Momma was putting stuff on my cuts and everything. She asked me why was my pants tied around my neck and why did I pee in em. I told her what Albert did to me and she said that I shouldn't bother him and make him mad like that. When I tried to tell her about Sabrina she told me to shut up and that I had too big an imagination for a kid my age. Then she made me put on some clean underwear and pants. She just walked outta my room. She told me to stay in there til she said I could come out."

Both detectives were stunned at what they had just heard. Jack looked at Maggie. Both had tears coming down their cheeks. "Are you ready to talk to Jessica?" Jack asked Maggie. Neither was ready but they were determined to get through this thing so they could begin processing the case.

The other daughter, 8 year old Jessica told a story pretty similar to Sabrina's. She had been molested but not penetrated. She was made to undress and then do things to Albert while he touched her all over. "Albert told me that I was really special. That's why he liked to take my clothes off and pretend that I was just a baby so he could hold me on his lap and pretend to change my diaper. Cept I didn't have no diaper, it was just pretend." "Did he ever hurt you when he played with you?" Maggie wanted to know how far 'the monster' had gone with this innocent little child. "As long as we just played the game and I did everything he told me to do he didn't hurt me. But sometimes I just didn't want to play cause I was sick or tired. He didn't like that. He said I made him sad when I didn't want to play with him. Then he would hit me on my legs or my back or my bottom. Sometimes he would pinch me really hard. That always made me cry. After he hit or pinched me he would say that he had to do that because I made him so sad. If I cried when he hit or pinched me he would keep doing it til I stopped crying. Then he would undress me and hug me and tell me how much better he felt now that I wasn't making him sad anymore."

"One day I told Momma about playing with Albert. I asked her if she ever played with Albert. She got really mad and wouldn't let me have anything to eat for three days. She said I needed to stop telling lies about Albert. She said if I ever said anything to anybody I would be very sorry."

"Now that Albert's dead I guess I can talk about it, right?" Both detectives felt almost glad that this ass hole was dead.

Several hours after they had been brought to the station Allicia was charged with child neglect, endangering her children and child prostitution. "You got nothing to prove any of this bullshit and you know it." she screamed as she was being booked and taken to the county lockup. She would be in court the next day to answer the charges before a grand jury. CPS (child protective services) was contacted. Once they arrived the children were put into their care and later placed in foster homes. They (CPS) didn't have a foster family that was licensed for four children who didn't already have at least one in their care at the time. The two boys went to the same family. The two girls were separated, each going to a different foster family. Arrangements were made for them to be reunited as soon as a family was found that could care for all four.

After the interrogations were finished Maggie and Jack each got a cup of coffee and sat at their desks. As they began the paperwork they discussed the case. Jack wondered "do you think we will find a motive for Al's death?" "Hard to say, but I wouldn't rule out Momma Allicia." Maggie replied.

The two detectives had been on the first case since just after midnight the previous Saturday night. Neither had gotten much sleep since. It was after six P.M. on Friday night when they got word of the second crime. This one involving the bodies of a male and a female. Their bodies had been found in what would eventually be the basement of a new home being built in a subdivision several miles east of the city. It was essentially a hole in the ground. The home was to have a basement so the only work that had been done was digging the hole for the basement. The basement walls had been framed. The footings and foundation had just been completed the day before.

Maggie was putting some new information into the computer regarding the first case when they got the call. She paused to ask Jack if he was ready to begin investigation on a new case. The expression on Jack's face gave her the answer. Even though they had been in homicide for several years, neither had grown accustomed to the terror, the horror that permeated each case.

They reported to the scene.

The two homicide detectives had their work cut out for them. Never before had they had multiple homicides at multiple locations. All within a period of about one week.

There didn't seem to be any correlation between the two cases. No motive. No suspects. No DNA left at either scene (other than that of the victims).

Who were these victims? Who wanted them dead? And why?

When they arrived the crowd was sparse. Nothing compared to the other crime scene. The subdivision was fairly new. There were only four houses in various stages of completion. Only one was completed and inhabited but the occupants were not at home. Jack's first thought was "they probably work in the city. They just haven't gotten home from work yet."

Since it was late October the weather would be changing soon. "Maybe when it starts getting cold outside some of this shit will stop. Or at least slow down." Jack was growing really tired of putting in so many hours. Even though he really didn't have a 'life' outside of work, he still wanted a few hours just to 'chill'.

A cursory check of the scene showed it was obvious that the two victims had been killed elsewhere. Their bodies literally 'dumped' in a hole. The Medical Examiner at the scene was reasonably sure both died from blunt force trauma to the skull. "I'll know more when I get a chance to examine them back at the lab. I would estimate time of death at about 12 hours or less. That would indicate that they were killed early this morning and their bodies dumped just after darkness fell upon the quiet community."

After the bodies had been removed everybody left except two uniformed officers in their police vehicle. There would be a 'police presence' on the scene until daybreak. Maggie and Jack stayed on the scene a little longer. There were tire tracks leading to where the foundation had been completed. As Jack shined his flashlight around he said "these don't appear to be truck tire tracks. More like a car or possibly a S.U.V. There's no sign of blood, hair, nothing. Not even a trace in the ground where they may have been dragged. My guess is that each was thrown into the hole from the vehicle. The vehicle had been backed right up to the hole. That would suggest two people. One holding the feet and the other the hands or arms. And just like a large sack of potatoes; grab, swing, toss. The victims are now resting in someone's future basement." After looking for herself, Maggie agreed with how they were placed there.

Just as the detectives were preparing to leave, a car entered the subdivision and stopped at the crime scene. "What's with all the yellow tape stuff strung up around that house? What's with the cop car?" the driver of the car questioned. Before answering, Jack asked "do you live around here?" "Yes, of course. We live in that house there." The driver was pointing at the only completed house in the subdivision. "We're just getting home from work. Are you going to answer my question or not?" The driver wanted to know.

Knowing how much of an inconvenience and embarrassment it would be Maggie and Jack identified themselves as police officers and then asked each of the occupants of the car to please step out and keep their hands where they could be seen. Each was asked to show identification. They were then asked to drive up to their house and show proof that they did indeed live there. They complied. While standing on the front porch of this beautiful new home Maggie answered their questions. "You see, Mr. and Mrs. Jackson, there was a double homicide committed this evening… Before you start to think the worse, it doesn't appear that the crimes were committed at that unfinished house. We believe the bodies were just dumped there. They were probably killed somewhere in the city. The way we treated both of you was simply police procedure. We had to know that you lived here and were just arriving home. Jack, that is Detective Carlson, and I are very sorry if we frightened you in any way. By the way, I'm Maggie, Detective Maggie Donaldson and this is my partner, Jack Carlson. It would be very helpful to us if you kept an eye out for anyone who looks like they don't have any business in the area. Okay? The police vehicle you saw will remain there until daylight." As they were walking back to their car Maggie and Jack could hear the couple discussing the situation. Each displayed some concern for having moved out in the middle of nowhere. Maggie decided that she would give them a call from time to time. She would talk to the chief and see if he could have a police vehicle cruise by once in a while.

During the ride back to headquarters Jack looked at Maggie as if seeing her for the first time. Maggie was driving. They often took turns driving and it was Maggie's turn to drive. Maggie, realizing that Jack was staring at her slowed the vehicle down and looked at Jack. "What's wrong Jack? Do I have dirt on my face? I know my hair is a mess, but I've never seen you look at me this way. What the hell is going on?" She was so upset that she pulled the car into a vacant lot and stopped.

Unable to restrain himself Jack began to reveal some pent-up feelings. "Maggie, I know I have no right to look at you the way I just did. But the way you talked to the Jacksons back there, I don't know, I saw a softer side of you. And that day we were questioning Allicia's kids you spoke so softly and tenderly. Nothing like when we're interrogating a perp. I don't know, it just got to me. Then you hugged Sabrina and cried with her. I mean, what kind of cop does that? You know that my wife died just over three years ago. I haven't been in a relationship since my wife passed. I know that you and your husband are having some problems and, I don't know. Maggie, I think I may be falling in love with you. I'm sorry. I didn't plan for this moment. We've had a great relationship working together. We're a really good team. But…" Before he could utter another word Maggie interrupted him. "Jack, we've both been under a lot of stress lately and I can understand how you might be confused. I realize that you've been without an intimate relationship since well before Jane's death. I know that she suffered with cancer for over a year. I know that you spent every waking moment at her bedside during her last few weeks. That must have been a gut wrenching experience for you. And you're right, I am having problems at home. Thank God, like you, I don't have any children. Bob and I have been trying to work things out. We've been in counselling for over a year now. If I had to bet, I would bet that we get a divorce. Bob and I are very different. I should have seen that a long time ago. But you know what they say - 'love is blind.' On some level I am attracted to you but I can't even think about acting upon those feelings right now. Maybe someday after things get settled and my divorce is behind me I can re-visit **us**. But for now, we just have to keep our minds on our work. We have three homicides to solve."

Except for the occasional calls over the police scanner, the drive back to the station was done in complete silence.

The autopsy would reveal that the first victim had been drugged before being killed. "It appears to be digitalis. If given enough it would have stopped his heart. The blows to his head likely was done post-mortem. Like someone wanted us to think he had been attacked from behind. Maybe a robbery attempt. It's difficult to know for sure." The medical examiner seemed to be somewhat shaken at the thought that someone would strike a dead person in the head with enough force to cause that much damage. In the second case, fingerprints from the male and female victims identified them as Justin Taylor and Marlene Stark. They had been living together for just over eight years. Unlike the first victim they had been injected with digitalis **after** being beaten.

After a brief follow-up by the detectives, it appeared that the couple had two children together. Both children were deceased. C.O.D. was ruled S.I.D.S. (Crib Death) in both cases.

Back at headquarters Maggie and Jack began trying to catch up on the paper work that is involved in police business. Each of them was still working on the first case. Now they had to begin a file on the second case. They worked in silence. Jack was too embarrassed to speak about anything not work related. He thought to himself *'what the hell was I thinking? I may be falling in love with you. What a crock of shit! She must think I'm the dumbest guy on the planet.'*

Both began to ponder. Each case seems different. Two males and one female, all about the same age. All beaten practically to death, all given digitalis. The bodies were found in different areas of the city. First victim near the Coliseum and the other two better than 10 miles away on the far-east side. Jack broke the silence, "I'm finding it difficult to believe that there is anything that ties these cases together. Other than the Digitalis found in the blood of each victim there is nothing that ties them all together. But we can't let that stop us from doing our jobs. We'll get to the bottom of this. We have to. By the way, did I tell you that the chief wants the two of us to handle both cases? If there are any more homicides we get the pleasure of taking those on as well? Unless we can prove that there is no correlation between the first two murders. Hopefully, there won't be any more homicides or beatings or whatever. I really feel that we should find new partners as soon as these two cases are solved." Maggie didn't know how to respond to the idea of breaking up their partnership. "With just these two cases we'll be working our asses off. If there are more cases **we** should be the ones to work them. Don't plan any vacations in the near future. And don't even think about calling in sick." Maggie commanded.

"Yes ma'am," Jack replied with the usual smirk on his face. "Do you want to get some dinner and we can start working the double homicide? And when was the last time I called in sick?"

Even though Maggie had told Jack that they needed to put a lot of time into these cases she declined his offer to go to dinner. "I really have a lot to do at home and since we're going to be burning the midnight oil I would rather get a fresh start in the morning. We can meet for breakfast if you want."

"Hey no problem. But ya still gotta eat don't ya? I mean, I'm going to grab a bite and head straight home myself." Jack was trying not to be too 'pushy'.

They left in separate cars each saying goodnight to the other.

Maggie's husband Bob, a corporate lawyer has basically a nine to five work day. He has always found it difficult to understand why Maggie can't be home for dinner every evening. That was the primary reason she felt like she needed to go home and have dinner with her husband tonight. She planned to tell him that she would be working at least two homicide cases involving a lot of extra time. Hopefully, this won't arouse any suspicions of infidelity on Maggie's part. Time will tell.

The following morning, the two detectives met for breakfast before starting their day on the cases. Maggie shared her concern with Jack regarding her husband Bob's reaction when she told him she would be working a lot of hours. Bob's reaction to her was "so, just you and Jack working the cases together? How convenient." Maggie feared that this could have a negative impact on the outcome of the divorce. **Her** divorce from Bob was likely going to happen soon. But, for now, she and Jack must concentrate on their responsibilities to the public. They had crimes to solve….

End of Chapter One

CHAPTER TWO

The House Next Door

Just two weeks after the three homicides a call came in through a non-emergency number to the police. A Mrs. Spencer was calling. She lived in a very small town just outside of North Bend. The town's name is Overton. It's within the corporate limits of North Bend. Consequently the North Bend police have jurisdiction over the little town. Jack and Maggie were off to Overton. They arrived about 15 minutes later. Jack started to knock on the door when it was immediately opened from inside the house. Jack looked at Maggie and whispered *"think maybe she was watching us drive up and was standing at the door?"* Maggie nodded in the affirmative.

After the introductions Maggie began questioning Mrs. Spencer. There was no Mr. Spencer. "Oh hell, he left years ago. Good riddance, I say. I'm better off without the likes of that worthless…" Maggie interrupted, "So you live here alone? Now, can you tell me why you called the police?" Maggie asked. "Yes, I live here alone. So what? I called the cops 'cause I ain't seen hide nor hair of nobody over there (pointing to the house next door) for about a week now." Jack began to question Mrs. Spencer. "Can you tell us who lives there, how old they are, whether they have children. Maybe something about their habits. Was there ever any fighting, yelling, things like that?"

"Well, I don't know for sure what their last names is. Her last name is different from his. Her first name is Naomi and I think his is Russ, I don't know. They was fightin' all the time. Yellin' and screamin' way into the night. Them little babies would just cry and cry. I never did see them kids but I heard em' plenty a times. I don't think either Naomi or 'what's his name' ever worked. They was home all the time. Mostly drunk or stoned or something. They never spoke or nothin'. I just seen 'em come and go. But I ain't seen nobody for some time now. Are you gonna' check on 'em?"

"Yes Mrs. Spencer. We're going over there right now." Maggie assured her. "You can just call me Gertie. My name's Gertrude, but I like being called Gertie." "Okay Gertie. Thanks for your help." Maggie wanted to comply with Mrs. Spencer's wishes. She (Gertie) might be a useful witness in the future. Right now, she's the **only** witness.

At the house next door the front door was locked but there was an odor coming from the house that didn't give the detectives a good feeling about what they would find inside the house when they entered. "Police, open up!" Jack shouted twice. After there was no response he kicked the door open and both he and Maggie had to back up and cover their nose and mouth. Without going any further they called the M.E.'s office. They told him to make sure they brought some Vick's Vaporub. This was typically used to block the odor of rotting bodies, etc.

The M.E.'s team found two bodies inside. One male and one female. There didn't appear to be any sign of foul play. No blood. No bruises or lacerations on either of the decomposing bodies. The really strange thing was that the two corpses were the only occupants of the house. No babies, no kids. Where were these babies that Gertie was telling them about?

An autopsy was performed on both victims. The cause of death was determined to be alcohol/drug overdose. "I need to run some toxicology tests but my best guess is that these two mixed crack with Jack Daniels. In large quantities, not a good thing. I'll know more in the morning." The medical examiner was one of the best in the state. Maggie and Jack were really thankful that they had Dr. Fields on their team.

Since there was no apparent homicide the case was closed as far as the death of the man and woman. However, more needed to be known about the alleged children. The case was turned over to Missing Persons.

The case was assigned to a "missing person's team". Their investigation began. The team was Barry Cartwright and James (Jimmie) Erickson. They had only worked together for a few months. Each of their former partners had retired. Barry had been assigned to robbery just two years out of the academy. He had worked robbery for a year. Jimmie had been on the force for almost eighteen years. He had done just about everything. He had been on missing persons for the past five years.

First stop, of course, Gertie's house. She repeated the same thing she had told Jack and Maggie. She was visibly shaken after hearing that the couple was dead. "What about them little kids? Who's gonna take care of em?" Gertie wanted to know. Jimmie asked Gertie "are you **sure** there were kids living there? Did you ever actually **see** them?" "No, but I heard em plenty. Crying and fussin all day and most of the night. Like I told those other cops, I ain't seen nobody for....... Wait a minute, I did see a car over there about a week ago. I didn't see nobody get out of the car.

I was lookin out my front window. That's when I seen the car. It was a dark car, black or maybe dark blue, kinda new. Well anyway I heard the car doors shut and that's when I went to the window. I stood there for a little while waitin for em to come back out. I had put the tea kettle on earlier and when it went to whistling I went to the kitchen to turn off the burner and take the pot off. I was gonna come back later to get my tea. Wouldn't ya know it? By the time I got back to the window all I seen was the car pulling out and turnin left onto the road. So I guess I ain't helped ya none." Jimmie wanted to make sure they got everything from Gertie that would be pertinent to the case. "So you heard the car doors close, went to the window and saw the car. But by that time the occupant or occupants had already gone into the house. Then you went into the kitchen to take care of your tea pot and when you got back you saw the car pulling out onto the road. Is that about it?" "That's about it. Wish I could help you more. Wish I had seen who was in that car and what they was wantin. You know, there is one more thing. Now I could be wrong. But it seems to me that since the day I seen that car I haven't heard them kids a squawking as much. Maybe not at all. I need to do some more thinkin. I got your cards and the cards from them other cops so I'll call one of ya if I think about anything more." Jimmie did have one more request for Gertie. "Thanks Gertie, you've been a lot of help. But while you're thinking about what you heard try to remember how many car doors you heard closing. Both the first time and then the second time, you know, before they drove away. That will give us some idea how many people went in and how many came out of that house." The detectives thanked Gertie and then went to look around the now empty, house.

The stench still lingered. There was no sign of toys, baby clothes or cribs. They did find several soiled Pampers that had been tossed out the back door into the yard. As much as they hated it, they bagged the diapers for DNA and fingerprints. "We need to get back to the office and see if they were able to ID the couple." Jimmie had never seen anything quite like this case.

Fortunately, both victims had been arrested numerous times. Mostly for public intoxication. They were both in 'the system'. The couple were Naomi Bartlett and Phil Stone. An address was recovered. The address belonged to Naomi's parents but no information could be found on Phil. He had a social security number but no record of ever filing any income taxes.

Naomi's parents lived about seventy miles away. Jimmie looked at his partner "looks like we're going on a road trip. Never been to that part of the state. Should be interesting…."

The detectives arrived at the Bartlett home about ninety minutes after leaving North Bend. It was Halloween Day. The weather was beginning to indicate an early winter. There was a real chill in the air as the two detectives got out of their car. The house was pretty run down and not very clean inside or outside. A man answered the knock on the screen door. "Whatta ya want?" Mr. Bartlett sounded rather rough and not too happy to have 'company.' Barry began the conversation. "Are you Mr. Bartlett, Carl Bartlett?" "Yeah, so what if I am?" "Is your wife home Mr. Bartlett?" By now Carl was getting pretty pissed. "Mr. Bartlett, I'm detective Barry Cartwright and this is my partner James Erickson. We're with the North Bend Police Department but we're here about a case that happened in Overton." Mrs. Bartlett came from the next room and asked what was going on. Jimmie asked if they had a daughter. "Is her name Naomi?" "Yes, but she don't live here no more. I think she lives up near where you're from. We ain't seen her in years. Is she in some kinda trouble? We don't have money to bail her out or pay for any lawyers." Mrs. Bartlett seemed upset just from the mention of her daughter's name. In an effort to calm her down, Barry said "Ma'am, it's nothing like that. Naomi is not in any trouble. I regret to inform you that she is dead and I'm sorry for your loss. She was found dead in her house with her friend Phil Stone." Without as much as a tear Mrs. Bartlett looked at Barry and then at Jimmie. "Get off my property. You didn't have to come all the way down here just to tell us our kid was dead. She started running away from home when she was still in grade school. Finally, when she turned sixteen she left for good. She came by here about five or six years ago. She had some guy with her and was asking for money. We sent her packin'. Told her not to bother us again. Guess she won't be now."

"Do you know if Naomi had any children?" Jimmie asked. "She didn't have none with her when we seen her five, six years ago. She coulda' had two or three by now." The detectives thanked the Bartletts and began the return trip to headquarters.

The house where the two bodies were found was searched thoroughly. There were only a few sets of fingerprints found. Two sets belonged to the deceased. None of the others were on file with any local, state or federal agencies. The same with DNA. Two matches on the couple and no other samples matched anybody in the system. Vomit, urine and feces samples along with some of the DNA collected came from someone very young.

Could these samples represent the 'kids' that Gertie heard coming from that house? The DNA from the excrement matched both of the adults. The missing children did belong to the couple. Blood samples from the couple and feces from the diapers confirmed it. The autopsy on Naomi showed that she had given birth at least once, maybe more.....

There were no leads, no suspects, nothing to go on.

The case was getting cold. Very Cold.

End of Chapter Two

****

Love's eluded me in the darkness of the night.

My heart's been torn to pieces.

My Spirit's taken flight.

Now I'm just too tired to continue with this fight.

Life has won its game; soon I'll take my life.

****

Dedicated to the many unfortunate people who have reached what they feel to be "the end". Beaten down and abused there doesn't seem to be any answers to their plight.

CHAPTER THREE

More Cases, More Terror

The "Overton Case", as it came to be known, wasn't the only thing that was getting cold. The weather in North Bend was changing. It was November 16th, just a couple of weeks before Thanksgiving and about two weeks since the Missing Persons Team (Erickson and Cartwright) had interviewed Gertie and the parents of Naomi Bartlett.

Yet another body turned up. This one, a female, was found just outside of a women's shelter downtown. Maggie and Jack were called to the scene. It was around 10PM and neither of them had retired for the day. Maggie and Bob had separated and Maggie now lived alone.

It seems as though Bob found something to occupy his time while Maggie was working 12-15 hours a day. It wasn't exactly some**thing**, it was some**one**. Even though Bob complained about Maggie rarely being home for dinner and even indicated he was suspicious of Maggie and Jack's relationship, he actually took advantage of the situation. He had been 'seeing' a law clerk from his firm. Bob admitted to the affair at the height of one of his and Maggie's arguments. Bob moved in with his 'girlfriend' the next day. It appeared that the divorce would not be contested. Maggie could have the house and one of the cars. The house had been paid off the year before. Maggie would not have to make a mortgage payment. Since there is no alimony in their state and no kids involved it won't cost Bob anything except the house and car. They agreed that Bob would pay the legal fees.

Jack typically didn't go to bed until after midnight. Maggie hadn't slept well since the separation. They were both awake and responded within minutes of the call. They arrived at the scene at about the same time.

Like the first two cases, the scene was filled with cops and reporters. Since it was still 'early' in the evening, several on-lookers had gathered.

"Okay, what have we got?" Jack addressed his question to a uniformed cop who seemed to have taken charge of the scene. He and Jack knew each other. "Hey, how you doing Jack? This is a really weird one. A couple was walking to their car from the theater. They thought she was sleeping on the street and tried to wake her up and help her into the shelter. As soon as the guy touched her he knew she was dead. They stepped away from the body and called 911 on their cell." "So what's so weird about that? I mean people die on the street all the time. You should know that."

"You're a cop for crying out loud." Jack was starting to lose patience with his uniformed friend. Maggie stepped in, knowing that Jack was under a lot of stress – both on the job and off.

"You'll have to excuse my partner. He isn't very patient. He just wants to get down to the facts. So what can you tell us? Start with from the time you arrived on the scene." The uniformed officer breathed a sigh of relief knowing he wasn't going to get his head chewed off by Jack. "Well, like I was trying to tell Jack, I just thought it was kind of weird that she was laying just outside the front door of the shelter. You know, with it being so cold and all. And she is just wearing a pair of sweats and covered with a light blanket. So why do you suppose she didn't knock on the door or something?"

As Maggie was talking with the officer the M.E. arrived. His name is Dr. John Fields. He had been the medical examiner for the city for over ten years. When he isn't examining dead people and crime scenes he is working at the hospital. He is chief of surgery there. He is really good at his job.

"Maggie, Jack, I'm glad to see that we have two of North Bend's finest working the case. So what do we have?" Out of respect for the uniformed officer, Maggie and Jack let him fill the doctor in with what he knew about the case.

"You know, it's pretty cold out tonight but the temperature is in the upper 30's to the lower 40's. That's uncomfortable if you're sitting outside watching a football game or taking a walk. But, it's really not cold enough to freeze to death. Without further examining the body I can tell you that she didn't freeze to death out here." Doc, as he was known by most of the people in law enforcement, began to examine the body. The detectives and officers (by now there were about half a dozen cops) stepped back to give Doc room to work. The 'uniforms' kept the on-lookers a good distance from the body. After about 10 minutes Doc had all he needed for now. More would be determined by the autopsy.

"Like I stated earlier, she didn't die here. And who goes out, downtown no less, without underwear? She doesn't have anything on under her sweat suit. She is barefooted no less. There's no blood, no ligature marks, no bruises, nothing. It doesn't even look like she put up any sort of resistance.

The only thing I could find that was somewhat questionable was some strange marks on both of her index fingers. Well the bus (ambulance) is here. I'll have her taken to the morgue and have my assistant start the preliminary stuff. Let you know as soon as I learn any more. How many of these things are we going to see before it all stops? This is not at all normal for North Bend. I've been doing this for a relatively long time and have not experienced this many deaths in such a short period of time. Talk to you all tomorrow sometime." Doc drove away followed by the 'bus.'

The autopsy and toxicology testing gave Doc and the police no further information. The cause of death would be 'hypothermia of unknown origin'. The police were not willing to close the case and were going to treat it as a homicide. One of the really strange things that they discovered was that there was no sign of the victim's fingerprints on the sweat suit. As a matter of fact, there were **no** fingerprints on the garment. She had been dressed **after** she froze to death. They still needed a name to put on the Death Certificate. The usual protocol is to take a picture (head shot) of the victim and circulate the picture throughout the city. It only took two days before they got a hit. An anonymous call was made from a pay phone. The call came in at the main desk of the North Bend Police Department. The caller said she knew the person to be Phyllis Harper. She didn't know the exact address but gave the police an area. The caller said that Phyllis lived about two blocks east of Central High. Central High (CHS) is a public school in a blighted area of the city.

It was no surprise to anyone that the case was assigned to Maggie and Jack. After talking to just about everyone within four blocks of CHS they finally located the home of Phyllis Harper. She lived at 8109 East

16th street. After knocking several times, there was no answer. Without knowing where Phyllis died they would need a warrant before entering.

Two days later a teacher at Abraham Lincoln Middle School reported one of her students hadn't been to school for several days. The 'missing' girl's name - Amanda Harper, her address – 8109 East 16th street.

By now the detectives had the search warrant and returned to the house on 16th street.

Even though they had a warrant they knocked, announced themselves as police officers and proceeded to kick the door open. Both wore latex gloves (normal police procedure) as they entered the house. Other than lots of junk – candy wrappers, cereal boxes, milk containers, spoiled food, soiled laundry and both dog and cat feces and urine all over the place everything seemed to be in order.

The house consisted of two bedrooms, a kitchen and what appeared to be the living room. The furniture was old and torn. There was the stench of cat and dog waste everywhere. Not to mention animal hair all over the place.

The detectives began the walkthrough of the house, taking extra precaution where they stepped. They found two dogs and several cats. Animal control was called to take care of the dogs and cats.

"Jack, come look at this." Maggie called from just outside the bedrooms. "Look at this Jack, there is a lock on the **outside** of this room." They entered the room and were shocked at what they found…………..

Maggie "maybe it's time to have a talk with the teacher at Lincoln Middle School."

The two detectives arrived at the school later that afternoon. School would be dismissed in about 15 minutes. They entered the school and went straight to the school office. "Excuse me, can you tell me who the teacher is for Amanda Harper?" Maggie asked the rather pleasant, friendly lady behind the counter. "Let me check, but I'm pretty sure that it's Ms. Fitzgerald. Yes, here it is. She's in room 202. It would probably be best if you waited until the children are excused from classes. Can I let her know who wants to speak with her?" "We're here from the North Bend Police department. Before you assume anything, Ms. Fitzgerald is not in any trouble. We just need to ask her about one of her students. And yes, we will wait until the students are dismissed." Jack replied.

After five more minutes the bell rang and soon the hallways were flooded with children. Most were following the instructions given by the teachers and principle to stay in line and exit in an orderly manner.

When it seemed that almost all of the children had exited the building, boarding buses or waiting cars the detectives made their way to room 202.

Ms. Fitzgerald was a very young, pleasant woman. She greeted them rather warmly, having known the purpose of their visit. "You're here about Amanda Harper, am I right?" "Yes we are Ms. Fitzgerald." Both detectives replied almost in perfect sync with each other. "Please call me Ann. Only my students refer to me as Ms. Fitzgerald. What can I tell you about Amanda?"

"What sort of student is she? Did you ever notice anything out of the ordinary, regarding her behavior? What about physical signs of abuse, that sort of thing?" Jack really wanted to learn as much as he could from possibly the only person who really knows Amanda.

"You've asked a lot of questions. I'll try to answer as well as possible. First of all, she is a very good student, a great kid. She's missed more than her share of school. Her personality is generally quite pleasant except for when she returns to school after an absence of a day or so. She seems to become very introverted, doesn't talk much, she seems really sad. As far as physical signs, I did notice that on occasion her skin seemed sort of discolored and she seemed like she was cold most of the time, even on days when it was warm and pleasant outside. When I quizzed her on these things she would reply with something like 'my mom's the same way, it must be genetic.' As far as bruises the only ones I saw were on her arms. However, our school nurse reported that she observed bruises on her back and legs. Amanda told the nurse that she had fallen several times, claiming to just being a clumsy kid. Is there something that you're not telling me? Have you found Amanda?"

Maggie responded "Ann, we have not found her but we did find her mother. Her body was discovered just outside of a women's shelter downtown. Did Amanda ever speak about relatives, grandparents, aunts, uncles?"

"I'm so sorry to hear about her mother. Was it murder or do you know? As far as I know, and you can check with the school office if you like, Amanda didn't have any relatives other than her mother. I'm sorry I can't be more helpful."

Jack, "you've been a great help. I wish we could tell you more but it is an on-going investigation. We'll be in touch. In the meantime, if you think of anything that might be helpful please contact us. Here is my card and Detective Donaldson will give you hers on the way out. Thanks again."

The detectives returned to their car and started the trip back to HQ.

End of Chapter Three

****

Lord above give me the strength,

To deal with the things I cannot take.

Give me the courage to find your love,

Give me the power to see you above.

Give me the insight to know what to do,

To know I can always speak to you.

Help me Lord to find my way,

Out of the dark, into the day.

****

Dedicated to anyone reading this book who may be a victim of domestic violence.

CHAPTER FOUR

Meet Mark

My name is Mark Gibson. I feel it's necessary to tell you that I am writing this from prison. I'm serving a ten year sentence. The reason that I'm in prison will be revealed later. I have a friend who I met several years ago. He is a writer and has been published several times. His name is Michael J. He has never written anything like my story before but after I told him what it was about it piqued his interest.

Michael is allowed to visit me once every other week. I try to write down as much as I can and then during his visit I read it to him and he takes notes. The guards watch us pretty closely. Everything that he writes down is scrutinized by the guards. They rarely say anything about what they have read.

In addition to the visits, I am allowed to call him. He records our conversations and transcribes them into the 'book'. I have two more years to serve as long as I don't do anything stupid. Our plan is to pretty much have the book finished prior to my release. I will go over it with Michael and send it off to our publisher. When you read this book I will be a free man! Thank God!

My wife Carol and I have three children – all grown and on their own now. I grew up in a poor family in what one might consider a ghetto or 'the hood'. Today it is considered to be one of the city's several 'war zones'. Unfortunately, not much has changed. If anything, it's gotten worse. Back in my day, shootings, theft, fighting, screaming, vandalism, arson were regular occurrences. I belonged to a gang for a few years (Jr. High/ High School). After seeing many of our friends being arrested and sent to Juvenile Detention, or worse I decided that gang life was not for me. It only made things worse.

I wasn't the only one who felt that way. Two other kids Herbert and Gilbert felt the same way about things. We formed our own 'gang' of three. We all grew up in the same area of the city. We were never more than three blocks from each other. We had known each other since as far back as any of us could recall. I even have vague recollections of kindergarten class with Gill at good old George Washington Elementary. Gill and I attended kindergarten in the morning while Herb's mom sent him in the afternoon. Kids attended kindergarten just half a day back then.

When we got into high school we began to change our view of the world. It wasn't that we felt we were better than the other kids. We just didn't want to spend time behind bars or end up stabbed or possibly shot. All three of us stayed out of trouble (at least we didn't get caught), we studied hard, got good grades. We graduated from high school and each of us went straight into the military. The G.I. Bill was still available so our college was mostly paid for. **If** we served Uncle Sam first. Herbert (Herb) joined the Navy, Gilbert (Gill) joined the Marines and I joined the Air Force. I chose the Air Force because that's the branch of service my brother had served in. Gill, Herb and I all went to Northwestern University on the G.I. Bill and graduated together four years later.

Gill went on to medical school after college. Herb became a firefighter/medic and I went on to law school. We stayed in contact through the years.

None of us moved away from the city. We agreed to get together at least one evening a week. Our wives never knew each other until they met at each of our weddings. Herb didn't have any brothers so I was his best man. Both Gill and I chose our older brothers for the honor. But if we didn't serve as best man we were groomsmen. Needless to say, we were tight.

Both Herb and Gill were born in North Bend. I was born in Chicago but my parents moved to North Bend when I was just three years old. I don't have any memories of my school days that don't include Herb and Gill. We all went to the same elementary school (K-6th grade), Jr. High School (7th and 8th grades) and finally high school (9th – 12th grades). There was only one year (from Kindergarten through college) that the three of us were not together.

My parents separated during the summer after I finished the sixth grade. I, along with two of my sisters, one who is four years younger than me, and one who is 3 years older than me went to live with my Mom. Two of my sisters stayed with my Dad. My oldest sister was married and lived in Atlanta. My brother joined the Air Force.

We didn't have any luggage or suit cases so Mom told us to put any clothes and 'things' we wanted into a shopping bag. We left, the four of us, each with our personal stuff in shopping bags. We spent three days at my Mom's cousin's house. She only lived a few blocks from our house.

My mom quit her job at the hospital and decided to move to Atlanta. We were to live with my sister and her husband until we could find a place of our own. My sister had been living there for a couple of years. Her husband was in the Air Force. My mom was convinced that she could get a job at a hospital in Atlanta and we could find our own place as soon as she got her first paycheck.

The day before we were to board the Greyhound for Atlanta my mother gave my younger sister and me a cigar box. She instructed us to go throughout our neighborhood and hand each neighbor a letter that my mother had handwritten. The letter said that my dad had been beating my mom and all three of us kids (not true) and she was going to have to leave to protect us. She was asking each person who read the letter to please consider putting some money into the cigar box so she would have enough to buy tickets to get us to Atlanta.

To this day, I don't know how much we collected. I only know that the next day my father refused to take us to the bus station. Mom didn't want to spend the money on taxi fare so we walked the mile and a half to the Greyhound bus station. It was a hot late June day and by the time we reached the station we were all drenched in perspiration.

Mom bought three one-way tickets to Atlanta and we sat on wooden benches waiting for the bus bound for Atlanta. I was eleven at the time, my little sister was seven and my other sister was 14. We waited a long time for the bus to come for us.

When we arrived in Atlanta the next day my oldest sister and her husband were there to pick us up. They had lived there for almost two years. They were renting an apartment on the third floor of an old brick house. The house was practically completely covered in some kind of ivy. It had a front porch on the first floor and balconies on the second and third floors. Living on the third floor our balcony was not covered like the ones on the first and second floor. The first two floors were larger than the third so in addition to the balcony at the front of the apartment we had a place to play in back by climbing out the kitchen window. The window opened up onto the tin roof covering the second floor apartment. There was no shade in the front or back of the house but we had several large trees on either side. There was a banana tree in the corner of the back yard. With no air conditioning and all of us sleeping in one room it got a little warm that summer. Sleeping was something that didn't happen very often. I probably slept more under the banana tree during the warm Georgia afternoons than I did on my 'bed' on the floor of my mom and sisters' room.

The job that my mom thought she had secured prior to leaving North Bend didn't develop so we spent that whole summer with absolutely no income. My sister and her husband were barely getting by on his military pay. My 14 year old sister got a job at a soda fountain but she barely made enough to help out with the rent. To 'supplement' my Mom made a cardboard sign for my younger sister and me to hold up as we stood outside the little market down the street. To this day, when I see someone 'panhandling' or whatever you want to call it I try to give them something even if it's the loose change in my pocket. I don't ponder why they are standing or sitting out there, I only know that it's not an easy thing to do. Some days my sister and I collected enough to have something to eat for supper. Sometimes we would have to decide whether we wanted to have supper or wait and have breakfast the next day. We never had more than one meal a day that year that we were in Atlanta.

It really isn't necessary to mention any of the other ways my mom was able to make a few bucks to put food on the table. It was just the four of us. My oldest sister worked at a hospital and had breakfast and lunch there.

My brother-in-law took his meals at the Air Force base where he was stationed. I don't recall a time when the six of us had a meal together.

After several months my dad starting writing to us and putting a few dollars in the envelope with the letter. I don't know how much we got in total during those months but I know it wasn't enough to buy much in the way of food.

For me, the bottom line in all of this is that I know first-hand what it's like to beg people for money. People you don't know and many who look down on you and threaten you if you don't leave the area immediately. I also know what it is like to go to bed so hungry that sleep evades you. Many nights the combination of hunger and the stifling heat and humidity caused me to literally cry myself to sleep.

The last letter I got from my father was in late August. We had been away for just over a year. I had spent my 7th grade without my two best friends. In the letter my Dad asked me to bring my sisters and come back to North Bend. He reminded us that school would be starting back up soon and we wouldn't want to miss the first day. My little sister would be in the second grade, my other sister would be in her second year of high school and I would be in the 8th grade. My last year of Jr. High.

Dad wrote out the directions for how to make a collect telephone call and said that if we decided to come home he would send us the money for tickets. Two days later, using the landlady's phone on the first floor of our 'house' we made the call. My mom was very reluctant to return but knew she had no other choice. If my brother-in-law got shipped out (which he did just three weeks after we left) we would have no place to go. When the money arrived it wasn't enough for four tickets. My mother thought that dad had just miscalculated the total cost. My sister and I went back onto the streets to beg for money to 'save our mother's life'. It worked. We got more than enough for her ticket. We even had enough to buy two comic books, a coloring book, a box of 32 Crayola's for my little sister and me. We also bought two 'Teen Magazines' for my older sister and some snacks for our trip back home.

Even though Dad said he would pick us up at the station he didn't show. We waited for over an hour when we decided to walk. When we walked into the house my dad was sitting in the kitchen.

He jumped up, through a chair across the room and screamed "I only wanted my kids back. You could have stayed there forever as far as I'm concerned." He glared at my mother as he shouted those hurtful words.

He wouldn't let my mother into the house. To this day, it breaks my heart to see her sitting on the steps in front of the house sobbing almost uncontrollably. I went back into the house and got my sisters' and my shopping bags and walked out the back door. "Just where do you think you're going?" "I'm going with mom" I shouted back with my cracking, pubescent pre-teen voice.

While we were living in Atlanta my Dad was busy tainting my Mother's reputation. Her cousin that we stayed with before going to Atlanta refused to take us in. She said that she had heard some disturbing things about my Mom and didn't want us there in her home.

We spent that night at the home of my mother's friend. She (Mom's friend) had heard all of the trash talk but chose to ignore it. My Mom and she had worked together at the hospital. Within just a few days mom had gotten her job back at the hospital. The hospital was just two blocks from what was now referred to as Dad's house. My uncle (my Dad's brother) loaned my mom enough money for the first month's rent on a house nearby. My sisters and I lived with my Mom. Two other sisters stayed with my Dad. My oldest sister was still with her husband in the military, now living in Germany. My brother had joined the Air Force when things started falling apart between my parents. He was stationed somewhere in New Mexico.

I was back at my old school with one more year until High School. Herb, Gill and I were once again 'the gang of three'.

Our relationship continued over a span of many years. Herb, Gill and I met on a regular basis. Every week, same day, same time, same place. God, how I miss my two friends. I wish things could have been different. But as they say 'hindsight always seems to be better than foresight'. As you will see, the three of us play a very key role in the remainder of this book.

End of Chapter Four

CHAPTER FIVE

The Investigation Continues

The day after Maggie and Jack visited the house at 8109 East 16th Street, the detectives returned. Inside the room with the lock on the outside they found a bed with no sheets or blankets, a pair of handcuffs, belts, chains, a pot that had been used as a toilet and strangest of all – a large chest freezer. The freezer was empty. The detectives came to the conclusion that the victim had been placed in this freezer naked and frozen to death. Then she was dressed in the sweat suit and taken downtown to be dumped in front of the shelter. But who would do such a thing? And why? And where was her daughter?

Two weeks later, the day before Thanksgiving Day – a missing person report came in through 911. The man had not been seen since Halloween night. The caller, a female sounded very distraught.

Since this appeared to be just a missing person situation, the team of Erickson and Cartwright got the case.

The two detectives got the information from the 911 call center. All calls received are documented and recorded. After listening to the call and checking the log they found the name and address of the caller. They left immediately to pay her a visit.

The home was in an upscale part of the city. Each home was rather large and even though it was the day before Thanksgiving you could see that the lawns and surrounding landscape had been carefully maintained. The first snowfall melted days before and the grass was still a beautiful green throughout the neighborhood.

A woman answered the door. The detectives introduced themselves and stated their business. "I'm Helen Gibson. I called to report a missing person. My son has not been seen since Halloween night. Can you please help locate him? He's such a good boy and I'm afraid something terrible has happened to him." She began to cry, then asked the detectives to please come in and sit down. She offered them coffee, which they gladly accepted. The two detectives, with Mrs. Gibson's permission looked around while she prepared the refreshments. They only got as far as the living room and den when Helen returned.

"Mrs. Gibson, what can you tell us about your son? His name is John, is that correct?" Det. Erickson began the interview. Mrs. Gibson was quick to respond.

"That's correct, his name is John. But I've always called him Johnny. And please call me Helen. Johnny was what you might call 'a late bloomer'. He never had many friends in school, he kept pretty much to himself. He always got good grades and never caused any trouble. His father left us while Johnny was in college so when he finished college he continued to live with me."

It was Det. Cartwright who continued with the questions. "What did he study in college?" "He majored in English literature with a minor in art." Was Helen's reply. "You mentioned that he doesn't have many friends. What sort of things does he enjoy doing? Like hobbies, books, movies, that sort of thing?" Helen sipped her coffee then replied "you know, as strange as it may seem, I really don't know what he does in his spare time. He works at the library you know. They keep him pretty busy. He's the 'Head Librarian' so he has a lot of responsibility. Most of the time he goes to work, comes home for dinner and that's about it. We always have dinner at 6:30. By the time we finish dinner and clean things up it's close to 8 and I retire to my room. I like to read for an hour or so then go to sleep. I awake early so I can fix Johnny's breakfast and pack his lunch."

Erickson, "so you don't watch TV or anything like that after dinner?" Helen took another sip of coffee, "no we just have the one television and it's in Johnny's room. I think he might watch it some. But most of the time I think he's on that computer that's in his room."

The detectives finished their coffee and stood. Det. Cartwright asked "Helen, can you tell us why you waited more than three weeks to report your son was missing?" Helen was quick to respond. "Like I told you earlier, his father just walked out on us one day. I always feared that one day Johnny would do the same. That is, until I had time to really think about it. Johnny would never do that. He really resented his father having done so and I don't believe that he would repeat such behavior." Det. Cartwright thanked her for her honest response. "Do you mind if we look around some more? We really need to know more about Johnny before we begin our investigation. May we begin by visiting Johnny's room?" Helen put her cup down and stood. "Anything that will help find Johnny. Should I wait here or go with you in case you have questions?" "You can sit and relax. If we have questions we'll ask them when we're finished." The detectives continued their 'search'.

Erickson and Cartwright had already done a cursory look at the living room and den so they walked through the dining room and kitchen on their way to the stairs that led to the second floor. There were three bedrooms on the second floor, one was Helen's, one was a spare bedroom and the other belonged to the missing Johnny. Out of respect for Helen, they didn't enter her room. They took a fairly close look in the spare bedroom. Everything was very clean and fresh. They proceeded to Johnny's room.

What they found there was quite interesting. This room spoke volumes of who Johnny is and what Johnny liked. Possibly even what he did in his 'spare time'.

Cartwright – "do you remember shortly after we got here you commented on how nice Helen's house was? She said that it had gotten to be too much for her to keep it maintained and that she had a groundskeeper who took care of the outside and maid service for the inside. She said that she couldn't possibly expect Johnny to help because he worked so hard at the library."

Erickson – "yeah, so what are you getting at?"

Cartwright- "don't you see it? Helen went on to say that the only thing Johnny does is help with the dishes, do his own laundry and keep his room cleaned."

Erickson – "so nobody goes into Johnny's room, not even the maid service. They clean the whole house except for his room. Let's keep looking."

In his closet they found boxes filled with books, magazines and pictures. All involving pornography. Worse yet, child pornography. 'Kiddy Porn'.

They decided to hack into Johnny's computer. This is a skill that Barry learned when he was working as a detective in Robbery prior to joining the Missing Persons Squad. Besides, Barry was younger and kept up with the latest trends in technology.

What they discovered was not surprising. Particularly in light of what had already been discovered tucked away in Johnny's closet. He not only had hundreds of pictures but he had subscribed to several web sites known to consist of some extremely disgusting topics such as 'how to seduce a ten year old'. None of this solved the question of why Johnny was missing. It only told them more about what kind of person he is…. or **was.**

It seemed like it was time to let Helen know what her son has been doing in his spare time. But then, does she have to know now? The detectives decided to hold off for now.

They did tell her that they would need to take Johnny's computer and some of his 'correspondence' to their office in order to continue the investigation. They called for two other detectives to come and confiscate the computer, etc. while they continued to speak with Helen in her kitchen. She had no idea what was being taken into police custody. At least not yet.

Cartwright and Erickson continued going through the pictures, magazines, etc. as well as further searching the hard drive on Johnny's computer before the uniformed officers took it to headquarters. Next they would visit Johnny's workplace – the library.

A search warrant in hand, the detectives went to the library. They were permitted to search through Johnny's office including his computer. There was no sign of any pornographic material of any sort but what they found on his hard drive was very disturbing. There were a number of protected files on his hard drive. It would require a password to look at the contents. Barry was good but he couldn't hack into any of the files. They confiscated the computer and asked that Johnny's office be secured – nobody in or out.

Every employee and volunteer was interviewed over the next several days. Without exception they all said that Johnny was a quiet, hardworking guy. His immediate supervisor had given him positive performance evaluations every year. Johnny had worked at the library for five years.

It was the only job he had ever had. He went to work there right after graduating from college. He started out as an assistant and worked his way up to head librarian.

Back in the squad room a team of experts had discovered names, ages, addresses and pictures of hundreds of children. Boys and girls. All between the ages of 10-13.

It's now April 7th, nearly six months since the first murder. "I can't believe that we didn't have any new cases all winter." Jack was relieved but at the same time curious. "What are they, fair weather doers? We haven't had any new cases since the frozen chick back in November. The missing persons' guys had a case of the missing librarian the day before Thanksgiving."

Jack spoke too soon. That afternoon - another missing person – a female.

Just one month after that, more missing children…. Followed by two more bodies - a male and a female.

Two months later a man found beaten, but alive. He can't remember anything, only that he has a very strong desire to tell someone he is very sorry.

Four months pass and a male and female are found beaten, but alive. This time it was behind prison walls. Two prisons, two victims, on the very same day. The female died in the ICU. The male, just like the one four months earlier can't remember anything. He died before he could reveal any details. The two victims were related by marriage – they were Paul and Janet Nelson. Both doing 3 to 10 for extortion.

Just one week later…. Two more bodies, this time both female…. As strange as it may seem most of their hair was missing, almost as though it had been <u>pulled out!</u> One of the victims had a daughter – she was missing.

The two homicide detectives were working 12-16 hours a day. "There HAS to be some correlation. But what"? Maggie asked as she and Jack were still in the squad room after midnight on a Saturday night.

Jack yawned as he spoke "Maggie, would you like to go have a drink with me?" Maggie was somewhat surprised "Jack, you know that we have to maintain a strict working relationship. My divorce has been final for a month now but I'm not ready to get involved with anyone right now." Now it was Jack who was surprised "who said anything about a relationship? I just asked a friend, a co-worker, to go have a drink with me. That's fine. Forget that I asked. I promise I won't ask again." Maggie began to feel like she had just hurt her best friend. "Jack, I'm sorry. I'm really going through a difficult time right now. I mean, trying to adjust to single life again, being responsible for paying the bills, keeping things up around the house. I don't know." Jack snapped back at his partner and best friend. "What do you think it's been like for me since my wife died? I had to make the same adjustments. If you would just let me I could help you get through this. But you just keep me closed out. You act as though I'm an intruder rather than a friend. I give up. If you need me you know where I'm at 24/7." Maggie felt like she had been told exactly what she needed to hear. "Hey Jack, maybe we should go have that drink." They left the building in one car – Jack's. Maggie's car would remain in the police garage overnight.

The investigation continued…. More victims…. A male is found in an alley – he had been badly beaten ….. No memory, just lots of pain…. Who would do this and why???? He was taken to Central Hospital for examination. One of his complaints was that he had been having problems in the bedroom.

The E.R. doctor asked "what sort of problems are you having?" The patient's reply "well, I can't, you know…. I can't get it up. Lately, I don't have any interest in sex. It's like, I don't know, like I'm not a man anymore. And take a look at this, my balls are like marshmallows, you know, the little ones. I'm fat and I got boobs. What the hell is happening to me?"

After further examination it was determined that the patient was a victim of 'chemical castration'. He had been given a fairly powerful drug (MPA) that causes a dramatic change in the person's sex drive. This procedure is sometimes ordered by a judge to be performed on a convicted sex offender. It's usually done in prison. The idea being that once the perpetrator is released back into society he will no longer have the 'urge'.

With somewhat large amounts of injected testosterone the person might return to normal. Theoretically, this should be done fairly early in the chemical castration process. However, in addition to administering MPA someone had also injected into his scrotum a drug used on animals. In this case he was far beyond any hope. He is impotent and will remain that way.

The question for the investigators is who would have access to this drug and why? And how were they administering it to him?

Three males one 18 and the other two 17 are found beaten and 'drugged.' They all attended the same high school and were all on the football team.

Over the next three days two houses were burned to the ground. Each one was within close proximity to the home of one of the victims.

Bill Anderson, a member of the Arson Squad was given the case. He began his investigation immediately. He went to the scene of each house, or what was left of them. Bill had been doing this for a number of years and probably had more experience than anyone in the entire state. Prior to joining the arson squad he had been a firefighter/medic for eight years.

He spent several weeks either at the two scenes or in the lab. His conclusion – arson. From the burn patterns and the testing of many remnants left at the scene (parts of the floor, parts of the walls, bedding, clothing) there was no doubt that both fires were purposely set.

Now all that is left to do is find out who and why. Bill -"this is NOT going to be an easy case to solve." The houses were rentals and each one owned by a different person. Neither house was insured which ruled out the owners torching their house to collect insurance.

End of Chapter Five

CHAPTER SIX

The Police Commissioner, at the request (more like an <u>order</u>) from the mayor contacted the Commander of each of the three squads involved. In turn each of the Commanders 'convinced' the detectives under their command to "get off their respective asses and get to the bottom of the mess that has consumed the entire city since last year."

All three teams – Homicide, Missing Persons and Arson met to compare notes.

The consensus - "There <u>has</u> to be a connection. What are we missing? We've had our share of violence in the past. But nothing like this. And why now?"

The detectives suspected a 'Citizen's Coalition.' This group of locals has actually prevented a few crimes and occasionally assisted police in the capture of law breakers. But, they have never taken any action against law breakers or acts of violence of any sort ...... so far....

Since Jack and Maggie had been assigned to the case since last October when the first body was found they were asked to 'chair' the meeting.

Jack, "yes, you are all correct when you say that Maggie and I were involved from the get-go but this thing goes way deeper than homicide." The entire room agreed but most still felt that Jack and Maggie were the ones who are the most familiar with all aspects of the collective crimes.

"Well, I guess the best thing to do is to make a list of the crimes. If we do it in chronological order maybe we can figure out whether or not they are connected. But we need to rule out petty crimes like shop lifting, simple battery and all that stuff." Jack walked to the whiteboard at the front of the room with an erasable marker in hand.

"Okay, first there was the guy that was found last October. Just a few weeks before Halloween. Then there was the couple found in the basement of the unfinished house. Then ...." Jack continued until they had

41

a complete list of all major crimes reported from October of the previous year through November of this year. We're into our second year with this thing. The mayor, commissioner, the whole city are going to have our asses as well as our shields if we don't come up with something.

Jack started a list. It looked something like this:

- **The first victim** – Albert Millar, beaten to death.
- **The second and third victim** – Justin Taylor and Marlene Stark, blunt force trauma, bodies dumped in unfinished home.
- **Missing kids** – couple found dead in home. Neighbor claims there were children in the home, no sign of the children.
- **Frozen body** – Female, Phyllis Harper, found outside of shelter. Her daughter is missing.
- **Missing person** – Johnny Gibson, last seen by his mother, Helen Gibson on Halloween night. Porn found in his room and on his computers.
- **A report of a missing female**
- **Three children reported missing by school officials**
- **Two more bodies – one male, one female**
- **A male found beaten but alive. Can't remember, but is remorseful for something he feels he has done.**
- **Two killed in prison**
- **Two females – dead**
- **Another male found in an alley – chemical castration?**
- **Three males, football team mates – badly beaten.**
- **The fires**

14 cases, 11 deaths, several missing children, one missing man and five people badly beaten.

Jack laid down the marker and walked back toward his seat. Before he sat down, "well, there you have it. We don't know what the victims had in common, we don't know who the perpetrators are and we don't have motive one."

The room was silent for about a minute and then they began the discussion – case by case.

End of Chapter Six

****

How can I show you what is inside of me
You don't want to look, you refuse to see.

Why don't you listen to what I have to say?
When I start to talk, you turn away.

How do I show you my pain is real?
It cuts like a knife, causing wounds that don't heal.

You say you love me, but I know it's a lie,
Why should I care, why do I try?

I started to crumble, started to cry.
Deep inside I've already died

****

Dedicated to the victims in the cases listed above.

PART TWO

Foster Parenting

CHAPTER SEVEN

The Foster Parent Experience

Over a span of about twenty years Carol and I were foster parents to several children. We started with accepting babies into our home. Then we moved 'up' to toddlers, then elementary school children. Later, we had about eight teens in our home. It wasn't always easy trying to juggle both of our careers and try to do our best with not only our three girls but one or more foster kids as well. But, somehow, when there was a need, when we got the call, we found a way to make it work. We never turned down the opportunity to welcome 'one more kid' to our family.

However, over the years we became pretty cynical with regard to 'the system'. Too many times we witnessed 'system failure'. Kids being placed with the 'wrong' foster parents. The failure of sufficient information being passed on to the foster parents. There always seemed to be a lack of proper communications between Children's Services and the foster parents. Too often we were not given a complete history regarding health related problems – physical, mental, emotional information that would have aided us in dealing with our kids.

Finally, we gave up, certainly not on the kids, but on the bureaucracy, the 'system', the agency. Just the whole thing. We haven't been foster parents for over ten years now. The past five is due to my not being 'available'.

I will share more details regarding our foster parenting experience later in this book. But for now, suffice it to say that we had witnessed our share of violence, particularly domestic violence.

Please Note: Anytime during the reading of this book, but preferably when you've finished it, I would suggest that you spend a few moments reading **the <u>Discussion on Violence </u>in the Epilogue**. This could give you a better understanding of some terms that may, in turn give you more insight into this 'THING' called ***Violence.***

If you need help regarding domestic violence please contact one of the agencies that are equipped to help you.

Here are just a few:

>***End the Silence on Domestic Violence***
>***National Domestic Hotline @ 1-800-799-SAFE (7233)***
>***Dr. Phil has a lot of information on his web site – <u>www.DrPhil.com</u>***

Don't ever think that you are alone. There is always someone who will afford you the help that you need.

Some of Our 'Kids'

As I mentioned previously in this chapter, my wife and I provided a home to a number of children in need of a safe place. In need of a "family", someone upon whom they could place their trust. Someone who would not abuse them or mistreat them. Many of these children had been victims of sexual abuse. Some would never talk about what had happened to them. We NEVER asked. However, some seemed to feel that they needed to tell their story. Here are just a few of the situations shared with us by some of our foster children. All of them sweet, innocent children. None of whom deserved what was perpetrated upon them.

The babies - Obviously they couldn't 'tell' us what had happened to them but it was obvious from the signs of malnutrition, bruises on their little bodies and other signs. They had not been loved and nourished as they should have been. The parents, or very often parent – meaning the mother, didn't have the patience to deal with a baby. Often times, these mothers were never educated in child care. I find it interesting that young girls don't have any problem figuring out how to <u>make</u> a baby but don't have a clue regarding how to <u>care</u> for the baby once it's born. Sadly, to some it's a way of getting assistance from the city or county to help pay for the cost of rearing a child. Meanwhile the 'father' may not even know about the child. If he does know, he typically feels no obligation to participate in the child's care. I know of at least three cases where a guy has gotten two and sometimes as many as three women pregnant at about the same time. Often, he is unemployed, uneducated and just plain doesn't' give a damn about what he has done.

When it becomes impossible for the mother to no longer care for the baby or when she has neglected it to the extent that it is taken from her 'home' the baby is placed into a foster home until some resolution is reached. That's where we (my wife and I) and many other foster parents come into play. The problem is we are given **most** of the information regarding the short history of this little human being but we're powerless to do anything about it. More often than not, important information was withheld for one reason or the other.

As recent as today, I heard a report that a twenty two year old had a baby and dropped it in a nearby trash can. Luckily someone walked by and heard the baby crying. The baby is fine, umbilical cord still attached. The mother arrested the same day. She <u>may</u> do a little jail time but the baby one day will have to be told that her mother didn't want her and discarded her like a piece of garbage.

Hopefully, the foster parents will be told the whole story when they take this baby into their home. Will the birth mother try to see her baby? Probably. What are the foster parents' responsibility if she shows up on their doorstep one day?

As foster parents we were often not given enough background information on our 'kids'. Information that may have helped us to better understand why the child was so difficult to care for. Why he/she cried most of the time. Yet it's supposed to be our responsibility to do what the parents never did and that is to protect the child and keep him/her safe and clean and nourished. I won't go into outcomes but you can read the newspaper or hear the stories for yourself. The baby may be returned to the 'mother' since she has now learned how to care for it. Or perhaps, it's given over to the grandparents who were responsible for 'raising' the mother of the child. If I sound cynical it's because I am. Ignorance, like poverty often runs several generations deep. PLEASE, I'm not putting down poor people. I was a member of a very poor family myself. Seven kids living in a two bedroom house with no indoor plumbing and a coal/wood stove for heat. Parents separated as I stated earlier. But by the grace of God some of us survived.

To further illustrate the lack of information I will share this story......

We had done foster care for five infants, all with reasonably good outcomes. After taking a two month break we were asked to foster a 9 month old baby whose parents could no longer care for him. Our case worker said that the father of the baby, NOT the mother, would have visitation privileges. After having the baby in our home for two weeks we got a call from our social worker that the father would be at our home the next day to visit. He would be there at 2 PM and would be allowed a 2 hour supervised visit. The next day a man who was at least fifty years old rang the doorbell. When I answered the door I was a little surprised to see that the baby's dad was a little older than I expected. He introduced himself "Hi, I'm Danny's dad. Can I come in?" I invited him in and Carol brought the baby in. The baby immediately knew the guy and was taken into his arms. "You're probably wondering why Danny's dad is older than you expected. Well, technically I'm not his dad. I'm his grandfather. My son is his real father but he can't take care of another kid. He already has two and another one on the way. He never married any of the women and isn't married to the one who is expecting. They're just living together. One of his kid's is the same age as Danny. They were born just a week apart. He had two women knocked up at the same time. I don't know what went wrong. I have two sons. My oldest boy grew up to be a really good man. But this one..... I just don't know. My wife died when he was about seven and I've tried the best I could. Seems like once he became a teenager everything changed. Drugs, alcohol, sex, the whole thing. I knew my son had a girl pregnant. I wasn't surprised since he had done it before. We didn't know anything about Danny until his mother contacted me. She was seven months pregnant at the time and had been kicked out of her parents' home. With nowhere else to go she asked if she could come stay with me."

I had heard just about all I wanted to hear about Danny's biological 'parents'. I told the grandfather that I would give him and the baby some alone time. Even though we were told that the visits had to be monitored I left the room with Carol.

We could hear him crying all the way from our kitchen. Not the baby. The 'dad'. We went back into the living room and saw him holding the infant in his arms, close to his chest and crying and sobbing.

"Are you okay?" Carol was really concerned about this man's behavior. "I'm fine. It's just that..... Danny's mother ran off about two weeks ago. She came home one night and said she was pregnant again and was going to blame it on me." By now he was starting to get himself together. "What she didn't know was that I had a vasectomy shortly after my son was born. That was twenty-five years ago. I told her to leave but that she couldn't take the baby with her. She left and I called the police. I told them that my girlfriend left me and I couldn't take care of our kid. They sent someone out to my house from Child Protective Services. They took the baby because I had told the police that I couldn't take care of him. They haven't been able to locate her. Nobody except you folks knows that I'm not Danny's father."

At this point Carol and I were really incensed. We sat there, staring first at each other and then to the baby and his 'dad'. "I can't believe the CPS or police didn't investigate this further. I mean, if you hadn't told us what you just did, we wouldn't have had any idea of what we are dealing with here. Thanks, I don't even know your name." "It's Max and you're welcome."

We contacted our social worker at CPS. She was out so we had to leave her a message to contact us right away. We invited Max to stay as long as he wanted. Hopefully, Megan (our social worker) could come over while Max was here and we could get some things worked out. She never returned our call and Max stayed for another hour and left.

The next day Megan called to see how the visitation went. Carol answered the phone. "So you called just to see how the visitation went? Why didn't you return our call from yesterday? We need to talk and not over the phone. How soon can you get out here? Or if you prefer, Mark and I can come to your office." Megan agreed to come see us later in the day. We would be her last stop before she went home for the evening.

Needless to say, our meeting that evening was anything but cordial. Why hadn't she done her homework? Why we were not told the truth about who the father of Danny is? "The truth is, we were told by Max that he **was** the father. He was concerned that since Sherry, Danny's mother, was only seventeen at the time she became pregnant and Max was fifty-four that he would be charged with statutory rape even if the sex was consensual. At the time that we removed Danny from the home and placed him into your care this was the information we had. Later, when Max learned that Sherry was going to accuse him of being the father of the child she is now pregnant for he denied being the father of either child. We now know that to be true. Since Max had the vasectomy before Sherry was born he couldn't possibly be the father of either of these children. We were going to inform you of the truth and if you would allow it we would like to continue giving Max visitation rights."

We agreed to allow Max to see the baby as frequently and for as long as CPS would allow him to visit. We came to know Max as a man who had been through a lot. He had two sons who were almost complete opposites in the way they turned out as adults. He had lost his wife to cancer when she was only thirty-one. He had held the same job at the post office for almost thirty years. Over time, we began to think of Max as a friend and wanted to do whatever we could to help him. He loved little Danny so much and it broke our hearts every time they had to part.

After having Danny in our home for just over six months we asked for a meeting with Megan, her supervisor, Max, Carol and me. It took about two weeks to get it arranged but finally on a Monday afternoon in September we got our meeting. As the meeting began I spoke first. "Carol and I have really enjoyed our time with Danny in our home. He is now eighteen months old and calls us momma and daddy. This isn't anything we encouraged but something that just happens with these kids. We have also come to know Max very well.

On behalf of Max, we wanted to know what it would take to grant Max custody of Danny with possibility of adopting him." The room became very quiet. Megan's supervisor, who goes by the name of Mrs. Bower broke the silence. "So what is it, you no longer want this child in your home? Or is there something else going on here?" I was surprised at her reaction. "Why would you ask such a thing? I thought this whole thing was about what is best for the child. This should be the primary objective in every case. We have come to know Max and have seen that he is a good man. He loves Danny and wants to take care of him. Why wouldn't it be better for Danny to be with a blood relative who has the means to care for him as opposed to continue in a foster home? I mean we love Danny too and would be willing to have him in our home for however long it takes. But here is a grandfather who, in my opinion, would be very good for Danny." After I had spoken I had the feeling that I may have had more success talking to a blank wall. The room returned to silence as both Carol and Max began to weep.

Megan was the first to respond. "Mark, Carol, you have been two of the best foster parents that I have had the privilege of working with. The only problem is that while you have everything needed to care for and to love children you lack the knowledge of the law. While Max may be a good person, the fact remains that he lied to us about his true relationship with Danny. In addition to which he is a single person with no means of support from any other family member, aside from his eldest son. He has proven that he lacks the skills it takes to be a good parent just by the way his youngest son, Danny's father, has turned out. How do we know that Danny would grow up to be any different than his father?"

"I guess we don't know the answer to those questions. But there are a lot of things in this life that we don't know about. What I need to know now is where do we go from here? What else can be done to try and resolve this?" I was shocked and disappointed that I had failed so miserably in my attempt to do what I thought was best for all concerned.

Mrs. Bower began to speak. "First of all, I'm removing you from the case Megan. Your replacement will be responsible for placing Danny in a different foster home. In the meantime, I will petition the Juvenile Court to arrange a hearing with Judge Barbara Brown to consider the matter. But I have to say that it doesn't look very favorable for Max at this point. I have to refer you to the comments that Megan made earlier regarding Max's history of child rearing and so forth.

I will also inform Megan's replacement to change the visitation arrangements to two hours supervised visitation once a month until after Judge Brown has made her final decisions on this case. Now, if there is nothing further, this meeting is adjourned."

We left the Juvenile Court Center with Danny but were told that someone would be at our house the next day to pick him up and take him to his new foster home.

That's exactly what happened. The next day a young lady along with our 'friend' Mrs. Bower came to our home. "I hope there are no hard feelings about our meeting yesterday folks. Sometimes these cases become very complex and confusing. Seldom does anyone 'win'. Is the baby ready to go?" "Yes, of course Mrs. Bower. We've packed all of his clothes and toys. Mark will be happy to help you carry things out. But if you don't mind I would like to carry Danny out to your car." "Of course, as you wish." Was Mrs. Bower's reply. Carol and I hugged and kissed little Danny as Mrs. Bower placed him in the car seat. Before she could close the car door Danny began screaming like we had never witnessed before. "Mommy, Daddy. Don't wanna go bye bye! Mommy! Daddy!" We could still hear his crying as the car drove away.

A week later we got a call from Megan to tell us that she had resigned from CPS. "I just can't do this anymore. The judge ruled against Max's request and Max will not be allowed to see Danny again. The new foster parents are going to pursue adopting Danny. Oh, and as for Sherry, Danny's mother. She was found dead in a crack house. She bled to death after giving birth to a baby girl. The baby girl is in St. Agnes hospital in critical care – she is a 'crack baby'. I'll try to stay in touch. Please don't give up being foster parents. Not all cases are as messed up as this one."

We've never heard from Megan since. Max comes over for dinner once in a while. The last time he brought his eldest son, daughter-in-law and his really cute grandchildren. Two granddaughters and a grandson named Max.

We never had babies or even toddlers after that. Our next foster children were a brother and sister. The girl was eleven and the boy was eight. Theirs was a story not unlike many of the stories we had either heard of or personally encountered.

The brother and sister had the same mother but different fathers. There was a baby brother who had yet a different father. Their mother currently had a boyfriend whose baby she was carrying. The boyfriend was physically abusive to the boy and was suspected of sexually abusing the girl. Both children told authorities that the boyfriend tried to kill their baby brother. No charges were filed. After numerous police calls to the home (loud noise, screaming, furniture breaking) CPS finally got involved. After speaking with neighbors, teachers and others it became obvious there had been neglect and the three children were removed from the home. The girl and boy to our home. The baby to another home.

We had met with our new case worker several weeks before. Janet seemed like she would be just fine. She was pretty young and had only been with CPS a short time. This was her first job right out of college. She called us to say that she had two siblings for us – a boy and a girl. They had a baby brother who was going to a different foster home. We were licensed for as many as four, although we had never had more than three at a time. Janet was aware of the problem we had with our last case involving an infant and felt it might be better if we took just the two older kids. Although we didn't agree we accepted the two. They were Hispanic kids. Mom was illegal but supposedly all three children were born in the U.S. which made them legal. Mom was living with her boyfriend, also illegal. None of the kids belonged to him. He had been arrested twice on charges of conducting cock fights. He had only served one thirty day jail term. He had a history of violence. But then, so did their mother. There didn't seem to be any signs of sexual abuse. We were very thankful for that. Most of the physical abuse was on the part of their mother. Most of it directed toward the eleven year old girl. She told of the times when her mother would force her to stay home from school to babysit her little brother. Her mother needed the time to 'visit' her friends. It turned out that the boyfriend was prostituting his own girlfriend to support their drug habit. She would turn tricks sometimes during the day which meant that they need Maria to babysit rather than go to school. Other times she would do her 'thing' at night while he was at the cock fights. After both of them being up all night they needed Maria to stay home from school and babysit while they both slept. Maria told us of at least two occasions where she tried to sneak out and go to school only to be caught by either her mother or the boyfriend. Her punishment was always the same --she would be dragged up the stairs to the bedroom, often times, by her hair. She would cry every time she told about it. She said sometimes the headaches would last for several days. Cigarette burns was another usual punishment.

Jose' was burned several times but Maria was burned far more. This was usually a result of refusing to stay home from school. Most of the times they were burned on their buttocks so that the burns would typically not be seen. Although, on one occasion Maria was asked why she couldn't sit still in class. She revealed to her teacher that her butt was sore from the burns. The school nurse examined her and was shocked to see what had happened.

The kids came to us about a month after a new school year began. We got them enrolled in School No. 103 which was just a few blocks from our house. After some preliminary testing the school officials decided that the second grade would be appropriate for Jose' and the fourth for Maria. They told us that they would move them up or back once school got underway. It depended upon how well they adapted to their respective class levels. Jose' stayed in the second grade but Maria was moved up to the fifth grade. We were amazed that Maria tested so well in spite of all of the time she was absent from school. As time went by the kids adapted really well. Both in school and at home. The only problem we had was that a fight would occasionally break out between them. There were times when the fights became extremely physical. Maria seemed to enjoy drawing blood by scratching her brother. He usually resorted to punching her. We eventually got things worked out. As Christmas drew near we explained to them that only good little boys and girls were visited by Santa. This seemed to work, for the most part.

Our memories of that Christmas with our two little Hispanic kids is one of the best and at the same time one of the saddest that we can recall.

We always tried to treat our foster kids just like our own when it came to Christmas presents. I have to admit that both my wife and I usually go a little overboard in buying Christmas presents. Not so much for each other but for our kids. We always went to church on Christmas Eve. And tried to teach them the true meaning of Christmas but when it came to gifts we kind of lost it.

That particular Christmas we had our daughters attempt to pry from Maria and Jose' what they might like for Christmas. This was not a new tactic. We used the same thing with our three girls. Often times having two of them try to get the third to reveal their Christmas Wishes. Carol and I did the same with each other. After several weeks of spying and prying Carol and I got a pretty good idea of what our 'new kids' wanted for Christmas. It turns out, and this is really sad, neither of them had ever been allowed to celebrate Christmas.

They had never gotten anything for Christmas. With the exception of one year when a charitable organization brought a box of stuff along with some food. The dump they were currently living in was deplorable according to CPS.

We got five or six things for each of the foster kids just as we had always done for our girls. This didn't include new dresses and such.

Christmas morning arrived. Carol had the turkey in the oven and pies cooling on the stove.

The night before we had baked cookies and the whole family had gotten involved in decorating them. Maria and Jose' had a blast. So here it is Christmas morning. Normally our girls were awake before we were but they knew that they couldn't begin unwrapping gifts until Mom and Dad were up. They also knew that they were not allowed to enter our room to wake us. What they usually did was to make as much noise as would be tolerated in the hopes of waking us. Sometimes they would get the dog to barking. That usually did the trick. This year they figured that their numbers were stronger by two. Jose' had his own room and Maria shared a room with our youngest daughter.

Here was the plan (we found this out later): Angela, our oldest daughter would go into the girls' room, taking the dog with her. Then the four of them, along with the dog, would go into Jose's room each wearing a Halloween mask. They would put the dog under the covers with Jose' and then start making scary noises. Jose' would awaken feel something in his bed, hear the strange noises and then see the scary faces. It worked, well sort of. What none of us knew was Jose' was scared to death of masks of any kind. He began screaming like a frightened little girl which made the girls all scream which woke Carol and me up thinking that aliens had invaded the place. Bottom line – I grabbed the first thing I could get my hands on – a hair brush and rushed into Jose' room screaming "get the hell outa here!" The whole time flailing the hair brush in the air. Carol had placed herself a safe distance behind me so she could see the whole thing. The kids began to laugh while Carol was losing it from behind me. As soon as I realized what was going on I just looked at everybody and said "Merry Christmas you little buggers." This was followed by the pillow fight of the century.

After breakfast, the unwrapping of gifts began. This was not the first Christmas with foster kids at our house but it was certainly the wildest. Everyone tore into their gifts. Shouts of glee filled the whole house.

Jose' "wow, look, it's a fire truck that you can work with this battery thing." It was a RC (radio controlled vehicle). I began to gather all of the wrapping paper, being careful not to pick up any small gifts with the paper. Suddenly I stopped to look at Maria. She was holding her doll close to her chest and crying. Carol and I weren't too sure if she was too old for a doll but our intelligence information that came back from our 'spies' indicated that it was something she would like to have. With the doll still clutched close to her she sobbed "I've never had a doll baby before. This is my very first one." WOW. That's some powerful stuff.

The rest of that Christmas Day was filled with playing games. Eating lots of great food and playing in the snow.

That evening as Carol and I were making a final pass through the house making sure things had been picked up we went by the kids' rooms. Angie was writing in her journal, our other two daughters were playing a game. Maria was packing all of her gifts, including her doll back into their original containers. We then looked in on Jose' and he was doing the same thing. We called Maria into Jose's room. I just had to ask "Why are you packing all of your presents away?" Maria looked at me with those big dark eyes of hers "so you can put them away for the next kids you get. We'll probably be leaving here sometime and you guys will need these for the next kids." Carol could hardly contain herself "honey, these are <u>your</u> gifts to keep. We don't know how long you will be with us but if you do leave to go to another home those will go with you. Those are yours and Jose's forever." Carol and I hugged these two precious kids and tried very hard to cry as silently as we could. Later that night in the privacy of our own room we both broke down. I couldn't help but wonder why there is so much pain in this world and why are the innocent children often the recipients of such pain?

Just before the end of the school year Janet called to tell us that there was a couple who was interested in adopting both children. "What about their little brother?" I wondered. Janet replied "He was adopted a few months ago and the same couple are going to adopt his little sister." "His little sister?" Carol inquired. "The baby that their mom was pregnant for was taken as soon as it was born. Both parents are in prison."

We always tried to avoid having a double standard in our home so when we initially got new foster kids we sat them down with our three daughters and explained the 'house rules.'

Punishment **NEVER** involved spanking or any other form of physical contact. The only time anything physical was involved was for their own safety. We had two boys and one girl who had gotten a little out of hand and were threatening harm to themselves and had to be physically restrained. Jose' was one of the boys. He had gotten angry with his sister and lunged at her with a pair of scissors. I had to grab him from behind while Carol removed the scissors from his hand. While I had my arms around him I sort of dragged him to a chair and 'placed' him into the chair until I got his attention and was able to settle him down.

We had a 15 year old boy come to stay with us for a short time. His parents had been killed in an auto accident on their way home from church. Bobby had gone home with a friend to have lunch and then spend the afternoon 'shooting hoops'. Bobby's parents were the only occupants in the car. A pickup truck hauling dirt ran a red light and crashed into their car striking it on the driver's side, Bobby's dad was killed instantly while his mom lived just a couple of hours in the ICU at St. Joan's hospital.

Both of Bobby's parents grew up in various foster homes. Neither of them had siblings that they were aware of. Bobby was left with nobody to care for him. He was very close to his parents and the only friends he had were from school and from his church. He was especially close to several couples who had kids about Bobby's age. It was one of those couples whose home Bobby was visiting when he got word about his parents.

Since Bobby was a minor and had no relatives CPS sent him to a group home who took in kids until they could be placed in foster care. Bobby stayed in the group home until after the funerals. He came to our home just one day after his parents were buried. Fortunately, we were completely briefed on the situation. As a matter of fact, we attended the funerals.

For several days he stayed in his room. He only came out for meals. It was summer so he didn't have school for another month.

One Saturday I had asked him to come with me to the hardware store to get some things for repairs that had to be done around the house. I sort of bribed him by promising him to stop by a very popular burger joint for lunch. While we were having lunch he looked at me and said "hey Mark, I like your church but could I go to my own church tomorrow?"

Without giving it another thought I said "of course Bobby and I'm sorry that we haven't given you that opportunity before this." He had been with us for almost a month and we took him to our church without even thinking about how involved he had been at his own church. I felt like the worst foster dad in the world at that moment.

When we got home I called the family together for a quick meeting. "Tomorrow, instead of going to Trinity, we are all going to Bobby's church." The room became totally silent. Then Angie, our oldest child asked "do you mean that Community Church way out in the country?" "That's the one" was my reply. "Oh, okay" was Angie's short reply. Carol thought it was a great idea. Our other two daughters, April and Amy did their usual thing and followed the lead of their big sister. If it was cool with Angie then it was cool with them.

Bobby, of course, was beaming when he entered the church, his church. Several of his friends, including the one he was with the day his parents were killed came to hug him and tell him how glad they were to see him. Bobby beamed as he led us through the crowd, introducing us as his foster parents and his foster sisters. Wow, what a day!

Bobby was adopted by the parents of his best friend. They had started the process soon after the funerals for Bobby's parents. We knew about it and supported it 100%. The adoption took place just a few weeks after school started. Bobby's best friend is now his brother. Bobby's mom and dad are now two of Carol's and my best friends. Obviously, we switched churches. Not just to see Bobby but through Bobby, we made some great friends. We see Bobby every Sunday.

We had a thirteen year old young lady who came to stay with us just two weeks after Bobby left. Her name is Cindy. Her situation was nothing like Bobby's. Her mother was an alcoholic and had, it seemed, a new boyfriend every other week. We're not sure how true that is but we do know that she had never been married and had several men in her life. The most recent boyfriend had a thing for hitting women including thirteen year old girls. He also had a habit of getting into bed with little girls, including Cindy. She had been with us for about a week when one evening she broke down and started crying uncontrollably. Unfortunately for me, Carol and the girls were out shopping. Cindy didn't want to go so she stayed home with me. I was doing some paperwork in my office when I heard her crying. We had asked our two youngest girls if they would mind sharing a room so that Cindy could have her own. It was no surprise to Carol or me that they gladly agreed. We are so blessed with wonderful daughters.

Hearing Cindy really struck me in a way I can't describe. It was breaking my heart. I went to Cindy's room.

Her door was partly opened so I called to her to see if there was something I could do to help her. She asked me to come in. She had been crying so hard and so long that her eyes were almost swollen shut.

"What's wrong 'hon'?" I queried. "No boy is ever going to want me after what he (mom's boyfriend) did to me." I knew what she meant so I remained silent. I asked her permission to give her a hug and she practically knocked me down when she threw herself at me and sobbed. She held her arms around my neck and laid her head on my chest. I could feel her shaking as we just stood there. She cried so hard that the front of my shirt looked like someone had shot me with a 'Super Soaker'. After a few minutes I asked her to sit or lie down on the bed while I pulled a chair up next to her. "Cindy, don't you ever think that there won't be a nice young man out there who would be thrilled to know you. You are pretty, you're smart and you have a great personality when you're not down on yourself like you are right now." By now she had stopped crying but every few seconds I heard a soft, almost silent sob. "Do you want to talk about it? Or maybe you would like to wait for Carol to come home and talk with her?" "No, I want to talk to you. I feel safe with you. I've watched you with your daughters and you treat them like they're something really special." I didn't know what to say. "Cindy, that's because they **are** special. And so are you. I know a little bit about what you've been through and it's not right. It's not fair. Nobody should be treated like that. But honey, none of it is your fault. The blame goes completely to him and, sorry to say, to your mother. Right now you're too young to think about having a boyfriend. But in a few years you will be old enough to date and go to dances and parties. Right now, you have to heal from the hurt that's been placed upon you. When the time comes for you to date he, or no one for that matter, needs to know about what has happened to you. Today begins a brand new chapter in the life of Cindy."

Carol and the girls came home a short time later. By that time Cindy and I were engaged in a wicked game of, you guessed it, Candy Land. I don't think I will ever outgrow that game.

Cindy stayed with us through all of the court proceedings and was strong all the way through it. Her mother was sentenced to ten years for child abuse, contributing to rape plus a couple other unrelated charges. Her boyfriend got twelve to twenty for rape, etc. etc. Cindy was adopted by another couple from our church the day after her fourteenth birthday. Wow, what a party we had the day before she left us. After all it was her birthday!

In addition to what I have just revealed to you we had another girl who at fourteen and then again at fifteen that was forced to have abortions. Then there was the boy who was an alcoholic at the ripe old age of fifteen.

Another girl from a strict, but perverted military family. Then let me not forget our Foster daughter who contributed the poems that are scattered throughout this book. Hers is a story of two parents who didn't want or love each other. Unfortunately, that lack of love and concern spilled over into their relationship with their children. I cannot reveal most of the details that I would like to because of the possibility of someone close to the situation making an attempt to retaliate.

Suffice it to say that the toll taken on her life, and on the lives of many children, can and often is, extremely devastating. Tasha is still undergoing therapy for the damage that was done to her by both parents. However, she's a survivor. She is married, has 3 children and works in law enforcement in another state. She is one of only two of our 'kids' who regularly stays in contact with us. She still refers to us as Mom and Dad and is very much a part of our lives and family.

I could easily fill another book just with stories of our foster parenting experiences but I'm sure you see some of the results of bad parents and bad people in general.

End of Chapter Seven

CHAPTER EIGHT

Meeting of the Minds

After completing the list, the teams discussed the possibility of a common "theme". Then they went back and discussed case by case again. This time by applying the common theme.

Jack "Well, we probably have more information on the first case than we have on any of the other cases. We know the victim was violent, had molested at least two of his girlfriend's children. He had at least one prior for rape. I mean, Lord knows the guy deserved it. But who? His girlfriend certainly had reason. Allicia is awaiting her day in court on charges of child endangerment, prostitution and probably a host of other charges yet to be discovered. The kids all seem to be adjusting to foster care. But I'm really concerned about the two girls. Sexual assault can leave scars that sometimes never heal. The boys have a better chance of recovering from the physical abuse. I mean, who really knows the extent of the damage that was done in that 'home'?"

Maggie "The second case has far more questions than answers. We learned from DNA samples at the scene that they are the parents of the three children later reported by school officials just a few days after the bodies were discovered. After a thorough search of the couple's home there was evidence that no children lived there. However, there was no evidence of any foul play or violence having taken place in the home either." A thorough search revealed very little in the way of DNA or fingerprints that didn't belong to family members or friends. It was determined earlier that this couple had lost two children to S.I.D.S. The COD was still under suspicion. Could they have been expecting yet another child so they could claim even more life insurance? They made out pretty well with the first two. The couple had been drugged with 'digitalis' and then clubbed post-mortem. Why and who and where?

Jimmie Erickson spoke regarding the strange house in Overton. The case reported by neighbor 'you can just call me Gertie' Spencer. As reported earlier, the couple died of drug and alcohol overdose. Reason unknown. "Still no trace of the children but there is, in my opinion, about a 90% chance that they do exist. Question is where are they? Hell, we don't even know how old they are. We can only guess that it's a boy and a girl. This is our top priority along with trying to find John Gibson. We're working with SVU on this one since it appears that John-Boy is a pervert."

The case of the 'frozen woman' seemed to show child abuse as well. The freezer found in one of the rooms indicated that it was not only the possible place where the victim took her last breath but possibly an instrument of 'correction' used on one or more of her children. No fingerprints were found in the home but the theory was that she was frozen to death in the same freezer she had used on her daughter. Scratch marks inside the freezer indicated that she was still alive when placed into the freezer. She literally froze to death. The marks on each of her index fingers indicate that the killers used what we referred to as 'Chinese handcuffs'. They consisted of cylindrical objects made of a type of material similar to what is used to weave baskets. When these are placed on the fingers and the fingers are pulled in opposite directions it becomes impossible to remove them without someone relieving the pressure. This meant that she could not move very well since her hands had been placed behind her back. The scratch marks inside the freezer were probably from her toenails as she attempted to break free. What a terrible way to die.

At the scene where the body was found two sets of fingerprints were lifted from the body. The theory was that the victim was placed into the freezer naked then removed and dressed in the sweat suit. The perpetrators had probably used gloves up until the point of dressing the victim. Their gloves were removed so they could dress her. The prints were run through the system and didn't turn up any suspects. Once again, a question remained – where is her daughter.

Maggie had returned to the school where the victim's daughter had attended. Both she and Jack had met the girl's teacher earlier in the investigation. Ms. Fitzgerald (Ann) didn't have much more to add to what she had told Maggie and Jack earlier. Other than the fact that she has missed a lot of school. She also seems to have a cold most of the time. She is shy and often flinches when approached. It's as though she thinks she is going to be struck. There had been no complaints to CPS as far as she knew. Ann was beginning to get very upset – "Maybe I should have said something to the principal. Is there a problem? Do you know where Amanda is?"

"I'm afraid I can't discuss the situation in any detail. I can only tell you that her mother is deceased. We don't have any leads regarding Amanda's whereabouts. I'm sorry. I will keep you informed as we find out more." Maggie replied to the now, weeping teacher.

Jimmie Erickson had already spoken about the missing person's case regarding John Gibson.

The next case, the one regarding a missing woman. Jack reported on this case. "Even though this is a very sad situation, I'm happy to report that we were able to close this one late last evening. The victim was a wealthy lady whose nephew grew anxious to get his inheritance. So he iced the old gal, buried her right on her property. The neighbors reported seeing the nephew digging in a very carefully maintained section of the garden.

They became suspicious since the victim had just paid a professional gardener a large sum to get the garden in perfect order.

We arrested the nephew and after a few 'persuasive techniques' he sang like a canary. He's in holding awaiting the Grand Jury. I have no doubt that he'll go to trial."

The case of the male and female found in the park was so similar to the one of Justin Taylor and Marlene Stark. They were drugged then beaten. This time the bodies were dumped in the park. We did get one break however. We recovered two sets of prints. Both matching the ones found on the body of the 'ice lady'. Since they are not in the system we can only wait for a break. Jack "big problem now is – we got three more missing kids. I guess this is going to be added to Erickson and Cartwright's already overwhelming case load. Maggie and I will stay on the homicides, etc."

While Jack still 'had the floor' he continued with what they considered case #0509. A man had been found badly beaten and drugged. "This one really takes the prize. This guy was found barely alive and crying. He had been drugged with what we think was Rohypnol, the date rape drug. He couldn't remember anything. We think he may have been hypnotized while he was under because he keeps apologizing for what he has done. He couldn't remember her name but was really sorry that he raped and beat her.

Once again, this was fairly easy. That is to a point – the victim was found just three days ago. His fingerprints and DNA were all over her. She had been raped, sodomized, beaten, and humiliated because she was dumped, naked, and unconscious in a very public place. She woke up with several strangers starring at her naked body. The real question here is who gave this creep what he deserved?"

Jack reported that the murders behind prison bars was going to be very difficult to solve. Most prison murders are. Neither victim had any priors regarding domestic crimes. "The fact that it happened on the same day and the fact that they were husband and wife and given the fact that they were both doing time for extortion tells me it was a hit and nothing more. Right now, we're letting the feds handle it."

Maggie reported on the two female victims who had been given a rather strange hair do. "Their hair had not been cut. It had been pulled out by the roots.

They were still alive when this took place and then mercifully, they were strangled after being raped and sodomized. Fingerprints led us to their identity. They are lesbians who have a daughter. When we went to the residence we found eleven year old Angelic Everson. She was in terrible shape.

She was malnourished, dehydrated, bruises covered most of her body and about half of her hair was missing. We took her to St. Margaret's where she was thoroughly examined. The doctors advised us not to question her for a few days due to her precarious condition. We obliged, allowing Angelic to begin her recovery."

Maggie continued "Angelic told us that her 'moms' didn't like her very much. She admitted that she had a habit of putting her hair in her mouth at times." "When I got really nervous and thought they were going to put those things inside me I pulled my hair out and screamed. But that just made them really mad and they hurt me a lot." She could barely talk through the sobbing.

I spoke with the medical staff and Angelic had been sodomized and had burns and scarring on her genitals. This kid has been through hell. I have to say, those two 'victims' got everything they deserved. I don't feel the least bit sorry for them. I almost want to give the doers a medal when we find them.

The man found in an alley, badly beaten and in a great deal of pain also had no memory of what had happened to him. However, he had an even greater problem – he had been chemically castrated. The details are sketchy but it seems as though he had been given MPA over a period of time. Then he had been rendered unconscious and given the same drug used on cattle. This drug must be administered directly into the scrotum."

Jack reported "we are looking into every possible lead but we have to find someone who could have gotten possession of these drugs and knew how to administer them. The victim likely has committed one or more rapes so we're running down every reported rape that is still open. Once we find victims I think we'll have a better chance of finding the perp."

"Regarding the three football players, that was pretty easy. After questioning countless girls and fellow football players we found out why they got beat up. There's a group of guys at that school that look out for any fellow student who is bullied, pushed around and date raped. It wasn't hard to find them. The school is handling most of the work and the AG will do whatever legal things have to be done. The number of victims (rape victims) runs in the double digits. These guys have been busy playing more than just football."

Finally, the arson team, consisting of one person, Bill Anderson, reported that he has absolutely no leads regarding the houses that were burned. He suspects that they may have something to do with the football players. We'll know soon whether this was where these girls were taken to be raped. Time will tell.

Now that they had it all out in the open and a full report was sent to the Mayor and Commissioner the teams began to study the open cases. The consensus was that there was definitely something that ties them all together.

They agreed to meet on a regular basis. Possibly weekly. The Commissioner expected weekly reports regarding progress.

The problem they all had was that crime was not going to stop just because they had solved some of the cases. They had the answers to **WHY,** for the most part but still didn't know who was carrying out the murders, beatings, etc. etc. They were now down to about a dozen that were yet unsolved. Missing Persons had their hands full trying to find the missing children and adults. They were far from wrapping this thing up.

There were far too many questions that remained unanswered.

Still – No DNA, No fingerprints

End of Chapter Eight

CHAPTER NINE

The Confrontation

I had been following the murders, beatings, etc. almost from the beginning. Having lived in North Bend most of my life. Nothing like this had ever occurred. I take both of the local newspapers and watch the news on TV both morning and evening. There was very little that I didn't know about what was happening. However, like the police, I didn't really know why or who.

Prior to my weekly meeting with my two friends....

"*There is a correlation in all of this 'stuff' and if I can see it then why can't the authorities see what's going down?" At the time I didn't realize the authorities* **had** *come to some conclusions regarding the crimes. They just didn't know who was perpetrating these egregious acts.*" But I had a pretty good idea who **was** behind things going on in North Bend.

The Commissioner took out a full page in both local newspapers 'warnings' targeting anyone who was committing domestic violence at any level. They needed to know that they are at risk of being punished by unknown sources. The warning even went so far as to say that if they needed help in controlling their anger there would be counselors available to help them.

"What a bunch of **shit!!**" I thought. "What good is that going to do? We should be asking citizens to be more aware of this terrible crime against humanity. If you see it or even suspect it, tell the police." That's what I thought this full page announcement should have conveyed. But maybe it would have some impact.

I had begun to deduce *"These adults all had a history, or at least a purported history, of some form of domestic violence. The children who are missing probably were victims of abuse. I think I may have found our 'missing piece of the puzzle.' Little did I know that the cops had already figured out the **why** but not **who**. The difference was that I think I know **who** the 'doers' are."*

"Regarding the two female victims, I recall the news report detailing that particular incident. But what's up with the bodies of a male and female?"

"The two women near where three friends live and the 3 year old daughter of one of the women, beaten with a belt, hog tied, then thrown into a closet (not sure for how long). Reason – they couldn't get her to stop pulling her own hair out. The little girl probably has trichotillomania."

"What about the young boy who was murdered at the hands of his mother and her boyfriend because the child had hidden their 'stash'?"

All of these acts were reported in the newspapers and on television news.

We (Herb, Gill and I) usually have our weekly 'meeting' at a place called 'The Hideout'. The Hideout isn't anything other than a nice friendly neighborhood bar and grill. They have a couple of pool tables, dart boards and for the 'risk takers' a room in the back. In the room in the back you could almost always find a game (poker usually) in progress. We rarely visited the room in the back. But we did enjoy our share of burgers and beer and lots of pool. Herb usually won.

I'm not sure how we got on the subject but soon after we sat down to enjoy our first beer, 'it' came up. We've always agreed upon something needing to be done about the acts of violence taking place in our city. It seemed like domestic violence in particular was on the rise. Each of us experienced it first-hand growing up in the 'hood' and each of us had developed a genuine hatred toward violence of any kind. The cause of domestic violence was something none of us could ever wrap our minds around.

What causes one family member to turn on another? Why do so many women feel the need to have a man in their life? Especially one who abuses them and their children. It just didn't make any sense. We all also agreed that not enough was being done about it.

Herb and I began to play pool. We usually come up with a plan for two of us to play each other, then the winner plays the third guy etc. We've been known to play til midnight or after. Just after I broke to start the game, "hey Herb, I really have a HUGE problem. I could really use your help." I told Herb that I had been following very closely the murders, beatings, kidnappings etc. "As much as I hate to say it Herb, I think you may have had something to do with all of this."

"Well, you have every reason to suspect me. I, along with Gill pretty much had everything to do with most of what's going on. We were going to invite you to participate. But knowing you probably wouldn't have the stones to pull it off we decided to keep you out of the picture."

Herb continued with his reason for each incident from the first victim to the most recent. He told me how each one had been 'performed' and who helped with each 'case'. Then he stated that he and Gill had resolved to continue for as long as it takes.

Herb and I quit playing, laid our sticks on the table and sat back down with Gill. "We've been friends for most of our lives, but this is too big man. I'm not sure what I could possibly do to help. I mean, I've practiced law for more than thirty years but I've never defended anyone involved in a capital murder situation." There was a long pause as my two friends stared into each other's face. Gill remained silent. Tears began to flow. First from mine and then from Herb's and Gill's eyes. We must have looked pretty silly, three grown men crying in their beers. "I have several friends that handle criminal cases. I'll refer you to one of them. There is absolutely no way that you will ever get completely out of this. But maybe I can keep you from facing the death penalty."

"Too late for that, my brother. I'm afraid we've gone too far."

"Tell me why?"

Herb explained that he has been very passionate about the problem of domestic violence. He'd seen too many perpetrators walk after committing egregious crimes against their spouse and/or children. Something had to be done. Somebody had to 'take care of things.'

I asked "why didn't you just scare the hell out of them and leave them alive." Gill replied, "Well, Mark, we did use roofies at first. But they've been taken off the market. I used up what I had left. Then we started using Ambien. Twice we used Ketamine, which I got from a veterinarian friend.

Ketamine is a horse tranquilizer. On humans it just renders them helpless to move or to even scream. But they can still very much feel pain."

Herb spoke up, "Mark, it was never our intention to kill anybody. The two guys that we hired to 'take care of things' just got carried away. After they rendered the victims unconscious or helpless they couldn't help but take it further. As you know, they even raped and sodomized some of the females. We found these guys in a cheap bar down on the canal road. I gave them an unregistered cell phone and told them I might have some work for them. The night I met them I was in disguise. I had heard that those types hung out at that particular joint so I didn't want them to ever know who I was."

I asked, "So, how did your scheme work? I'm surprised your two goons didn't narc on you at some point." Herb, "they enjoyed their 'work' and the money too much. Besides, it would have been difficult for them to know either of us. When Gill and I had a 'mark' we would call the cell that I gave them. We would let them know who to hit and where to find them. We always dropped the money at a different place each time. When the job was done they would call us and then we would let them know where to pick up the money."

Gill, "Herb and I took turns calling them. We used a different phone each time. For each job we would give them a new phone along with the money. We would instruct them to incinerate their old phone."

Herb, "most of the time we would set the 'mark' up. We would make sure that they were at the location we had given our goons. Neither Gill nor I ever knew their names. We just referred to them as 'D' and 'D2'. They never knew what we meant by those names but Gill and I knew that it stood for 'Dumb' and 'Dumber'. We thought about 'G1' and 'G2' for 'Goon one' and 'Goon two' but decided on D and D2. Damn, they were stupid."

I was growing more and more curious. "What about the missing people? How did you pull that off?"

Herb was first to answer. "Gill has ties with a sort of 'underground' adoption agency. He simply filled the needs that he was made aware of. Every child went to a family who wanted children and who would care for them and love them like nobody had ever loved them before." Gill, "even though the couples had been checked out by the 'agency' I was working with I had them checked by a private detective to make absolutely sure they were right for the children. With the exception of a few, the kids were young enough that they wouldn't remember what they had been subjected to prior to being placed with their new family. Those that were older were counselled after we 'grabbed' them. We sort of 'reprogrammed' them. They all, without exception were happy to be out of the hell-hole they had been in. The old gal down in Overton? I think her name is Gertie, we slipped in there and talked to her neighbors. They were only too happy to give us their babies. We gave them 500 bucks, a case of whiskey and some 'weed' that we had gotten earlier from our two goons. Those kids were twin girls just nine months old. They were filthy, malnourished and really in need of being held and loved. The twins went to a couple who had been married for five years and unable to conceive. They both have great jobs and live in Seattle."

I was curious, "why did you refer to the two 'goons' in the past tense? Aren't they still working for you?"

Herb, "no, they got killed about a week ago in a car crash. The idiots had all the money they could possibly spend but they decided to knock off a Seven-Eleven. They were picked up on video and caught within two hours. The cops pulled them over and they tried to run. They ran their vehicle under a semi doing about eighty. They were both decapitated. We, that is Gill and I, recognized their pictures in the paper the day after it all went down."

I asked, "What are you going to do now?"

"That's easy, we're going to make sure nobody gets killed again and one or both of us are going to carry it out ourselves. In the meantime, we are looking for other like-minded people to join us. Hopefully we can persuade others to aid in our pursuit. I don't see that Gill and I can do what needs to be done without the aid of others. We've got three or four people that are interested."

I was shocked, "you guys have got to stop. I wish you hadn't told me anything about it. I could go to jail, lose my license, my family. You two would be finished. Gill would lose his license to practice medicine. Herb would be fired from the Fire Department and lose his pension. And me? I would go to jail for obstructing justice by withholding this information."

The meeting ended but I was really confused. *What in God's Name am I supposed to do with this information?*

End of Chapter Nine

CHAPTER TEN

No End to the Madness

Herb and Gill continued to carry out what they considered to be 'justice'. No one lost their life but many were hurt badly. Some to the point that they likely will not recover completely.

The three of us met several weeks after 'the confrontation' for a few beers and just to chat. However, I couldn't help but ask how 'things' were going.

Herb – "Well, as you probably know from the news, a few people have run into some 'problems'. But nobody has been killed for quite some time now."

"I know, but when are you guys going to give it up? You can't continue to be the judge, jury and executioner. The violence is not going to stop. At some point you two are going to have to face the fact that you're fighting a losing battle."

Gill – "That's where you're wrong Mark. The incidence of domestic violence in North Bend has dramatically decreased in the past six months. In fact, violence in general is on the way down. We've got these bastards scared. It's right where we want them."

Herb – "Gill and I have been doing most of the work but we have found three other people willing to aid in our quest. They have carried out a couple of the 'deeds'. But mostly, it's been Gill and me."

"Do you guys really think you're going to reach a point where you no longer have to 'carry out justice'? I mean, you will never run out of 'victims'."

Herb – "Victims? What the hell are you saying Mark? These scum bag dick heads aren't 'victims'. They're anything but that."

"Don't you see guys? They are, in every sense of the word, scum and everything. But they are scum to the people they are beating, raping and so forth. But once they commit the deed they become your victim. You guys target them, plan their punishment and carry it out. I mean, think about it! Man, I don't know. I can't keep quiet much longer. This is weighing way too heavy on me. Please stop. If for no other reason, stop on my behalf."

Gill – "The three of us have been friends like forever. I can't imagine life without you and Herb. But Herb, the three others, and I are on a quest. We have to continue until we draw our last breath. You can go ahead and turn us in but there will always be someone else to pick up the 'torch' and run with it."

"I suppose you're right Gill. I love you and Herb like brothers and I could never turn you in. You gotta do what you gotta do so I'll step back into the shadows and be a silent observer."

Herb and Gill – "Thanks."

In the meantime the detectives were still working the cases. They discovered that most, if not all of the victims of violence were themselves perpetrators. Their job now was to try and catch these 'vigilantes' in the act.

Jack to Maggie – "What we need to do is take a more pro-active approach. Let's try to watch for domestic violators, tail them and possibly catch the vigilantes when they attack." "That's a great idea Jack, but how are we supposed to know who these domestic violators are?" "Simple, we get the word out that if anyone is in a domestic violence situation they need to report it to the police. We will guarantee their protection and begin tailing the boyfriend, husband, brother, sister, mother, whoever."

Maggie – "We need to run this by the chief before doing anything else." Jack – "Why? What do we need to get his approval for? I mean if this thing works you and I will probably get a promotion." Maggie – "And if it doesn't work? Then what?" Jack– "How can it not work? All the victim or victims have to do is let us know and we will take it from there."

After the two goons were killed in the car crash robbery detectives went to their house. Since they died right after robbing the Seven Eleven the robbery detail needed to see if there were any signs of other crimes.

They found a lot of garbage. Bags from McDonalds, along with the paper the food had been wrapped in. Empty beer and soda cans. The place was a dump. They discovered several sweat suits that had been tossed into a basket in a closet. They were covered in blood stains. They also found two pair of shoes with blood stains. The strangest things they found were several unregistered cell phones.

At roll call the next day the robbery guys gave their report. Jack looked at Maggie, "do you suppose this has anything to do with our cases?" Maggie, "we need to get that stuff to the lab. We'll have them check for blood types along with DNA." Jack had a strange look on his face as he replied, "great idea Maggie. Next we need to try to get anything we can from the live victims. We may even have to exhume a body or two."

Jack and Maggie had gotten married two months after the 'big meeting'. They were in the process of adopting all four kids from the first case. Sabrina is now sixteen, Henry is eleven, Jessica is nine and little Harry is seven now. Maggie will tell you she doesn't know why but she and Jack just feel like it's the right thing to do. They both feel like they have a special bond with these kids. Jack had paid his house off with some of the insurance money he got as a result of Jane's death. Since Jane's death he never went anywhere, never did anything other than work and sleep. He had saved most of what he made as a police detective. Maggie and Jack sold their houses and together bought a bigger house out in the suburbs, not too far from where the bodies in the second case were found. Irony is a strange thing.......

Jack and Maggie continued to discuss their approach to the cases as they went forward toward finding the doers. Maggie – "Jack, are you listening to yourself? You're asking victims of domestic violence to all of a sudden get up the courage to turn in this person who has terrorized them for God knows how long. I mean, just because the cops say 'hey, it's ok now. Just turn the bastard in and we'll take care of you. Do you really think that they are actually going to do it? Come on Jack, you know better than that. And what happens if some woman who has been a victim for years decides she's had enough and turns the son-of-a-bitch in and then turns up dead herself? Who's gonna take the blame for that?"

Jack – "Damn, Maggie you are really putting the squash on my idea. Problem is, you're right. What was I thinking? It seemed so simple in my head. Then when I got it out and you picked it apart it really made me feel stupid. I apologize. Don't tell our soon-to-be kids that their soon-to-be dad is an idiot. Okay?"

Maggie – "You're secret's safe with me 'Daddy'."

Jack – "What are we going to do Maggie? We can't just continue spinning our wheels. Somebody out there has to know who these people are and what is motivating them to action. Problem is, we don't know who the people that might know who the people are….. Did I just say that?"

Maggie – "You're right Jack. If we can flush out anyone who might know anything at all about who these people are it will be a giant step toward wrapping this thing up."

Jack – "Okay. As much as I hate to say it, we need to split up. Oh, I don't mean split up on a personal level. We need to split up as partners. One of us can work on trying to figure out where the domestic violence is likely taking place. The other person can work on finding out who knows what about the vigilantes."

Jack and Maggie began working their separate areas. They decide Maggie would be best suited for seeking out the domestic violence. She would be hanging out at grocery stores, food pantries, laundry mats, shelters and the like. Jack will hang out at the bars and clubs, including The Hideout.

The following Monday they got the lab reports back on both DNA and blood. The two guys who 'lost their heads' during the police chase had indeed committed at least some of the beatings. They decided not to exhume any bodies. Medical records from the deceased gave them enough evidence regarding blood type and in one case DNA. These guys had carried out some of the crimes. But why? Both Jack and Maggie agreed that they didn't act alone. For one thing, there didn't seem to be anything missing from the homes of the victims. And then there were those cell phones….

It was Saturday. I hadn't met with Gill and Herb for several weeks. I called to see if they were available to meet. I wanted to make sure they weren't 'working'. They both agreed to meet with me.

"I've been thinking a lot lately about you guys and I just wanted you both to know that no matter how much I am against what you're doing I would **never** report you." Gill – "Thanks Mark, that really means a lot to me and I'm sure Herb here feels the same way." Herb – "I never thought for a second that you would ever narc on us. It's just that it really bothers me to see how it has affected you." I told them what I had heard on the government building grapevine regarding the two guys killed in the police chase. Herb, "how are they going to link us to what these guys were doing? Anyone could have hired them to do what they did. All the cops have are those cell phones. There's no way they can be traced back to Gill or me." We had a few beers, talked about the old days, the old neighborhood and after a couple of hours parted ways. We agreed to meet every other Saturday at six.

Maggie was having far more success than Jack was. She had overheard a couple of women talking about the abuse they were getting from their significant other. She managed to get names and addresses of some of the women and shared them with Jack. "So what do we do with this information Maggie?" "I don't know Jack. But these women are clearly being abused." Jack didn't know how to respond. "A big part of me wants to take these bastards out myself. I'm beginning to see what may be causing the rage in the vigilantes." By now, Jack and Maggie referred to the people carrying out the deeds on the violators as the vigilantes. The recipients of the vigilantes' rage are to be referred to as the 'violators'. The 'victims' are obvious.

Maggie – "I can't blow my cover and approach any of these victims but I really want to let them know that they don't have to put up with the abuse. But how do I convince them of this without blowing my cover? It still comes down to finding either a vigilante or someone who knows who one of them is."

Jack – "Now that I have names and addresses of 'potential violators' I can start tailing them. Perhaps I can be a witness to one or more of the vigilantes carrying out their form of 'justice'."

In the meantime, the chief assigned another pair of detectives to follow up on who may have hired the two dead guys.

Two weeks later the three of us met at The Hideout. "So how's it going guys? Have you been 'working' lately?" Herb – "Mark, you know you don't want to have the answer to that." "Just thought I would ask. I mean just because I don't agree doesn't mean that I don't care about you guys."

Gill – "Truth is Mark, we took care of business twice this week. You may have read about it or seen it in the news. Two of the 'recipients' of our 'service' are upstanding citizens in the community. Problem is, they were abusing their two daughters. He was sexually abusing them and she was punishing them for crying and complaining about 'Daddy'. Neither of them will ever be interested in sex again. I won't go into details but trust me on this one. As far as their daughters go, they will never see them again. They are in a safe place now. Just as we have done with many other kids in the past year or so."

"Damn, Gill. You and Herb are really playing hardball here. I've wondered about all of the missing children. How they're doing in their new homes. How their new parents are adapting. Let's order a round. You guys hungry? I'm gonna order a nice big juicy cheeseburger. You guys want one?"

Herb – "You go ahead Mark. We can drink another beer with you but then we gotta go." "Shit Herb. You mean to tell me that beating the hell out of some prick or drugging some asshole is more important than our friendship?" Gill – "Back off Mark. We don't pick the time or place. 'They' do. It just so happens that we have two 'ladies' that need to be taught a lesson."

"I can't believe you guys wail on women like that." Herb – "Mark, it ain't just men who do these ugly acts. A certain percent are females. We don't discriminate." "What are you going to do to them?" Gill – "If you must know, I got a new supply of Rohypnol. After we administer the 'roofies' they won't know what hit em." "I can't believe I'm hearing this. Are you going to rape them, sodomize them, what? I mean this just doesn't sound like you." Herb – "If you knew what these two did to two little boys you would want to string em up yourself. Trust me." "Hey, I don't wanna know. In fact I'm gonna drink my beer, eat my cheeseburger and you guys go do what you gotta do. Just don't tell me any more stuff." Herb and Gill finished their beers and left.

While I was finishing my burger I glanced over at the bar and saw a familiar face. *"Where have I seen this guy? It's that detective, what's his name? Jack something. He's working the cases that my 'friends' have created. I've seen him and his partner on TV. Wonder what he's doing here? I don't want to make eye contact with him. I know, I'll pretend to be talking on my cell.*

I'll finish my burger and beer and then quietly make my exit. I gotta warn the guys."

Knowing they were 'busy' I called Herb's cell and left a message for him to call me ASAP. He didn't call me back until the next day. I told him who I saw at The Hideout. I suggested that we start meeting at a different place from now on. Herb just laughed. "Mark, this guy doesn't know me or Gill or anyone. He's probably just drinking a beer at the taxpayers' expense."

We still planned to meet at The Hideout in two weeks. I decided to go there a little more frequently by myself just to see if this Jack dude shows again. I went there on a Wednesday evening and there he was with his partner. *"This is getting serious. Then again, it's a public place. He has a right to be here same as me." I'm not sure why all of a sudden I was filled with guilt. I hadn't done anything. Then I thought to myself, "I haven't done anything but I know who has. I gotta quit coming here."* I didn't say anything to Gill or Herb about seeing the detective and his partner at The Hideout that evening. Two days later I decided to have lunch at The Rendezvous. It's similar to The Hideout but a little more upscale. I was sitting there enjoying a nice chicken salad sandwich when 'he' walked in. He glanced my way and I pretended I didn't see him. I finished my sandwich and got out of there.

When our regular 'Saturday at six' rolled around we met, as usual, at The Hideout. I refused to discuss anything about their (business). We shot some pool, drank a few beers, just like old times. Apparently Gill and Herb didn't have to take care of anything that evening because they stayed the whole evening. We really had a great time. Just the three of us. I didn't see 'my friend' that evening but I was expecting him at any moment.

End of Chapter Ten

CHAPTER ELEVEN

Jack & Maggie's Private Life

Jack and Maggie were working their respective 'areas' with very little success. At last, a quiet evening at home. This may possibly be the last quiet moment they would have for a while. The kids were coming the next day. The children had visited three other times per the CPS guidelines. They wanted to make sure the kids would adjust without any problems before they begin the adoption process. The only thing Maggie feared was the possibility of being reminded of that horrible night just over a year ago when the kids spent most of the night at headquarters. In the previous visits it hadn't come up so perhaps she was just over-thinking the situation. Maggie – "Jack, do you think we'll be good parents?" "It's a little late to be asking that isn't it? I mean tomorrow we will be one huge step closer to being the parents of four kids." "I know Jack, but I can't help being concerned. I mean Sabrina is in high school. She's sixteen years old. Are we ready for that?" "Maggie, you need to take a Xanax or something. You're starting to make me nervous."

"Sorry Jack. Let's talk about the case. Have you gotten any leads from the bars and clubs?" "No, not really. I did see the same guy at two different bars. Probably a coincidence. Other than that, nothing. How about you?" "No, I still see the same women at the same places. I feel like they may be getting suspicious of my hanging around. I mean I'm trying to fit in. I buy stuff at the grocery store. I get things at the shelter and food pantries so that I look like I'm on their level. I secretly send things back to the shelter and food pantries later. I try to dress down so I fit in. At first the women seemed to really open up to me but here lately not so much." Jack – "You need to chill baby. I think it's good that you will be taking some time off when the kids come. Maybe that will give you a new perspective." "You're probably right honey. It's just that I haven't worked undercover for a long time. I feel really self-conscious. Like everyone can see right through my cover." Jack – "Strange as it might seem, what if we switched assignments after you go back to work? I can hang out at the laundry joints and beauty parlors and all that. You can go to the bars and clubs…. Just kidding."

The plan was for Maggie to stay home with the kids for about 2 months to make sure they were settled in. Her mother was coming from L.A. later to stay until they find a suitable nanny.

Neither Jack nor Maggie had ever been a parent before now. Most couples start out with one or two. They were beginning their adventure in parenting with four children.

Their new house has six bedrooms. At the time they bought it they weren't sure why they needed a six bedroom house. Now they knew. All six bedrooms were on the second floor. The largest one was, of course, the master bedroom. Jack and Maggie had been sleeping in it since they got married. When it became apparent that they would have the four kids they cashed in a few CD's to pay for furniture for four of the other five bedrooms. The sixth bedroom was furnished to be a study. They also bought several new outfits of clothes for each of the kids. They would take them shopping later so that they could pick out clothes more to their individual tastes.

Maggie – "Jack, I'm a little nervous about owning such a big house. I mean, I know we need the space but how do you think it's going to look. Two cops living in this big house on our salaries? They're going to think we're on the take or something." "Who the hell is 'they'? We don't have to explain anything to anyone. You know and I know that we put everything we had into this house. Now, I may have to get a part-time job to pay for the utilities and upkeep. But, what the hell, it's ours. By ours, I mean you, me and the kids." Maggie – "I'm sorry that I even mentioned it Jack. You're right. We're going to be just fine."

Jack – "Well babe, I think we're prepared for our family." Maggie – I don't know what else we could have done. I mean, they each have their own room, plenty of clothes, good schools, and a nice house and of course, great parents." Jack – "We'll have to wait and see about the great parents thing. I'm still a little nervous on that subject. But we'll make it work. I'm sure. After all of the bad things that we've seen parents do to their kids? If anything, we'll probably be over-protective with ours."

The next day the kids arrived. Each was taken to their respective room. And Except for Sabrina they all seemed happy with the choice of clothes that Jack and Maggie had picked out for them. This was no surprise to Maggie. "I'm sorry Sabrina. I should have waited until you got here before picking out your clothes." "That's ok, uh.. Maggie. Should I call you Maggie?" "Well, that is my name. But I hope someday you'll feel comfortable calling me Mom. That's up to you."

Sabrina – "I really didn't mean anything negative about the clothes you bought me. I mean the pajamas and sweats will be fine. It's just that I don't really wear dresses much so…. Maggie- "That's fine. We'll save one of the dresses for church and take the others back and exchange for whatever you want."

Sabrina – "Church? You mean you expect us to go to church? We've never had to go to church before. I don't see why we have to start now."

Henry, Jessica and Harry all seemed delighted with their new clothes and were looking forward to shopping for more. As far as church, they all thought it would be kinda cool. They had never been and didn't know what to do when they got there but all were willing to give it a try. Sabrina, on the other hand, was going to be a challenge.

Jack – "Ok, enough of the talk about clothes and church and all that stuff. Come on, let me show you the rest of the house. Those times you visited you only saw the living room. Let's take a real tour." Jack and Maggie showed the kids the office/study complete with computer, printer and everything they would need to help them with their homework. All of the kids were impressed with the huge kitchen. Even Sabrina "I've been taking a cooking class in school. Maybe I can cook dinner sometime for the whole family." Shortly after she heard herself say 'the whole family' she immediately changed it to 'I mean all of us'.

The tour continued as the kids were shown the large family room where they would be permitted to entertain friends or just hang out together playing games or watching the 75" flat-screen TV.

The backyard was completely fenced in and the front yard carefully manicured. Jack's only rule was that they respect the front yard and try to keep it looking nice. The back yard contained a huge 'jungle Jim' thing, a climbing wall and a trampoline. The house came complete with a larger than normal heated swimming pool, complete with slide and diving board. All four of the kids, including Sabrina, were overwhelmed by all of the stuff that was now theirs.

The triple car garage would be a great place for Jack to teach the boys some fundamental things regarding tools and making minor repairs.

That evening Jack cooked steaks on the gas grill while the kids went for a swim. After a great meal Jack built a fire in the fire pit and they all sat around the fire and roasted marshmallows and made s'mores. They really had a great time for their first night.

After the kids were tucked in for the night Jack and Maggie heard little voices coming from Jessica's and Harry's rooms.

Jack – "What's wrong kids?" Harry – "I'm afraid." "Me too," was the reply coming from Jessica's room. Since it was their first night in a new house Jessica and Harry, ages nine and eleven were allowed to sleep with Jack and Maggie. About half-way through the night Jack decided to sleep in Harry's bed the rest of the night.

The next morning was Tuesday. The kids had just one more week of summer vacation left. Everyone was in the kitchen anxiously awaiting breakfast. That is everyone but Sabrina. Maggie went to check on Sabrina. "Hey, sleepy head. Are you going to join us for breakfast?" "Go away. I don't get up this early. I'll get up when I'm ready. And I don't do breakfast so you can….." She stopped herself before saying something she would regret. Maggie- "That's fine honey. I didn't do breakfast when I was your age either. And sometimes I slept until noon. We'll see you when you get up. Love you." Maggie went back downstairs.

While the five of them were enjoying a nice breakfast Sabrina came into the kitchen. She still had here pajamas on. "Good morning everybody." Wow, what a shock, especially for Maggie. "Good morning Sabrina, glad you could join us." Was Maggie's cheerful reply. Sabrina- "Yeah, well I couldn't sleep with all this yellin and laughing and besides I'm not that sleepy. Jack- "Are ya hungry? Got plenty and the pancakes are still warm. Come on. You can sit by Henry and me." Sabrina sat down but didn't say much. She seemed to enjoy the pancakes and actually smiled a few times at both Jack and Maggie.

At Maggie's direction each person had a responsibility regarding cleaning the kitchen and washing the dishes. She said that later she would have a schedule made up so that only two people would be responsible after each meal. That would free the others up to do homework, play or whatever. The list of duties would include her and Jack as well.

It was only ten o'clock when breakfast was finished and the kitchen cleaned and the dishes placed into the dishwasher.

There was plenty of time left in the day for each of the kids to begin acclimating themselves to their new home. But Maggie and Sabrina needed to have a heart-to-heart talk.

Maggie poured herself a cup of coffee and offered one to Sabrina. "No thanks. I just had a cup with breakfast. I'm not used to much more than that" was Sabrina's response. She started to leave the room. Maggie felt that this was an appropriate time for the two of them to talk. "Please sit down Sabrina. I really want to talk."

"I'm sorry Maggie. But I still have a lot of stuff to sort out in my mind. I've never had a relationship with a parent. It's always been me taking care of my younger brothers and sister. I've never had anyone to guide me or to even pretend to take care of me. Jack told me yesterday that my Mother had passed away in prison, she caught pneumonia or something and couldn't fight it off. The thing is, I didn't feel anything when he told me. I should have felt sad or something. She was my mom even if she mistreated us and made us feel like we were in the way. I can't even remember one time that she hugged me or told me she was sorry."

Maggie tried to console her, "Honey, what you are feeling is normal. But, you're right, she was your Mother. The funeral is tomorrow. I can get you excused from school so you can attend. It may give you some level of closure."

"Closure. You mean that everything will go away if I attend her funeral? All of the beatings, cigarette burns, pulled out hair, hot showers, being stripped naked in front of my mother's boyfriend and brothers and anyone else that might be around. I don't think so." Sabrina was very adamant about not attending the funeral.

Jack and Maggie gathered the others and asked if they had heard about their Mother's passing. Sabrina had told them last evening just after learning it herself. None of them had any interest in attending the funeral.

This was the first of many crises that Jack and Maggie would face with their family.

Jack- "You know Honey, the others are young enough that we can tell them that they are going and that's the end of it. We can take them for ice cream after." Maggie was a little taken aback by Jack's approach to the situation. "Jack, we can't just pack them in the car and drive off to the funeral of someone they haven't even seen for over a year now. We should let them forget her in their own way. Going to the funeral might conger up all sorts of bad memories." Jack felt like he had just been chastised by his Mother when he was a teenager. "You are so right Babe. I don't know what I was thinking. Let's see if we can get Mrs. Davis next door to keep an eye on them for a couple of hours and you and I can go to represent her 'family'. We can talk with the children when we return." They both agreed.

The funeral was sparsely attended. Two women from CPS were there, the assistant warden from the prison, one of the prison guards and a few of the police personnel that were involved in the case early on.

With the permission of the funeral home director Jack was permitted to take pictures of Allicia in her casket. At the gravesite Jack took a couple more pictures. He planned to bring the children to the site when they felt ready. It would be at that time when Jack would show them the pictures of Allicia in her casket and the graveside during the funeral process. As morbid as this all seems, it was just part of helping the children to adjust and hopefully begin to bring them closure regarding their 'past life'.

Over the next few weeks the kids were enrolled in school. Jessica (9) and Harry (7) were enrolled in Spring Valley Elementary. Henry (11) was enrolled in James Bradford Middle School. Sabrina (16) was enrolled in Thomas Jefferson High School. In the span of just a few weeks Sabrina had come a long way toward adjusting to her new home and new environment. She is really a sweet, caring sixteen year old.

Maggie's mom arrived, just as planned, on a Saturday, 2 days prior to the kids starting school on Monday. Maggie's mom's name is Margaret, the same as Maggie except that she prefers Margaret rather than Maggie. Whatever her reason, it didn't matter. It helped to tell them apart. Margaret was nothing like Maggie in the personality department. This turned out to be an asset as time went by. Margaret was just what the kids needed at this juncture in their getting adjusted. The ads for a nanny had been in the newspaper for several weeks but not too many "qualified" people had responded thus far.

Maggie's dad was an investment advisor in L.A. Many of his clients were Hollywood types. He was busy practically 24/7 so he really didn't have time to 'grieve' Margaret's absence. Although he did have his moments when he felt a little lonely.

With the ads placed for a nanny, Margaret settling in with the kids. With each child enrolled in their respective public schools it was time for Jack and Maggie to make plans for going back to work. Jack had taken the past two weeks off to help get everyone settled in. Both Jack and Maggie were impressed with the extent to which Margaret had gone to organize the "family". She had schedules for various responsibilities at home as well as all of their school activities.

All four, at Margaret's 'encouragement,' had gotten involved in sports as well as extra-curricular activities. The kids were really busy, no extra time to get into trouble. Maggie said that Margaret raised Maggie and her siblings the same way. Jack was really pleased with her approach.

Monday morning came too soon. Maggie and Jack returned to duty. Their four children to their respective schools. The song 'Monday, Monday' by the Mamas and the Papas was playing in Jack's head as he put on his suit jacket and tie for the first time in two weeks.

End of Chapter Eleven

PART THREE

The Beginning of the End

CHAPTER TWELVE

The Warning

I called Herb and Gill to arrange a meeting. We met at our usual place at about our usual time. I felt like I ought to give them a 'heads up' regarding what I knew. Or at least what I was pretty sure I knew.

I was a little pissed at how calm and collected my two best friends were acting. "Look, even though I don't practice criminal law, I still spend a lot of my time in and around the courts. The police headquarters is in the same building." "Yeah, so?" Herb questioned. "So I hear a lot of things. I frequently have coffee in the café in the Municipal Building. Occasionally, I meet with clients in the café. Mine is a very familiar face around there. As a matter of fact, I've seen some of the detectives who are working the cases. I recognized them from the many interviews they've done on television."

Once again, Gill joined the discussion. "So let me get this straight Mark. You occasionally have a cup of coffee in the same café as some of the cops working the 'case'. From this you're telling Herb and me to be careful because the cops are 'closing in on us'? Do you even know the names of any of these detectives?"

"As a matter of fact I do know some of their names. Like I told ya. I've been following this thing pretty closely. The two primary detectives are Jack and Maggie. I don't remember their last names. Look guys, why don't you take this opportunity to quit?"

The room suddenly seemed to be completely silent. The three friends parted ways without anything further being said.

Jack and Maggie were having lunch in the cafeteria in the Municipal Building. "Hey Maggie, I think I may have stumbled onto something."

Maggie put down her sandwich. "What is it?" "Well, do you remember the police chase that ended in the two guys crashing under a semi?" "That's been a while Jack. What did you come up with?" "I heard two burglary detectives who have been assigned to follow up on the case. They were saying that they found some interesting items in the apartment the two were renting. They found a ton of money, mostly cash, and several cell phones. They also found a bunch of notes with addresses, dates and times scribbled on them." Maggie was puzzled by Jack's apparent excitement about what had been discovered. She asked "what does any of this have to do with our case?" Jack was quick to respond. "I asked the detectives if I could look over the evidence that they found in the apartment. They called down to the evidence storage room and gave me permission to look over the notes and cell phones. Now, here's the interesting part – almost all of the dates and times coincide with dates and times when our cases occurred." Maggie still was not sure she followed where Jack was going with this. "So, what could these two robbers have to do with murder, beatings, rape and all of that stuff? I mean, they couldn't even pull off a robbery at a Seven-Eleven. They even pulled it off in broad daylight." Jack seemed to be surprised that his partner of several years and now his wife couldn't follow where he was going with his newly discovered evidence. "Don't you see Honey? This is the closest we've come to finding anything in the way of evidence. I think these two had something to do with what's been going on. My guess is that they were hired to carry out some of the beatings and murders. The notes were dates and times when they could carry out the 'deeds'. None of the addresses were places where bodies were found. They were probably places where the victims could be confronted." Maggie was beginning to pick up on what Jack was leading to. "Jack, I think you really have something here. Do you think the phones were used to make contact with the person or persons who were putting out the 'hits'?" "That's exactly what I think. Problem is we can't prove anything with the phones since they were prepaid phones except tracking where they were purchased. There's no data or history in them. My guess is that they used a different phone for each hit. They probably were instructed to destroy the phones but decided to collect them. It seems to me that they weren't too intelligent."

This is the closest the two detectives had come to begin closing at least some of the cases.

Unfortunately, Herb and Gill decided that there was no way out of what they had started. They would be more selective in deciding who they would target.

It was 'business as usual' for two more years. Beatings, people being drugged. For the most part, the victims provided very little information. They had been drugged and had only vague memories of going to a bar or restaurant or out to meet a friend. The only thing they could recall was waking up in the hospital. During this two year period there were no fatalities. The case was, again, starting to grow cold....

It was Saturday evening and I went to The Hideout to meet my two friends. Gill was there when I arrived. We waited until almost 9PM. I asked Gill, "did you and Herb have business tonight and you forgot about it? Is that the reason you're here and Herb isn't?" Gill looked puzzled, "hey Mark, if we had 'business' I would know. I just talked to Herb this morning and he said he would meet us here at the regular time. I don't know what's holding him up. I'll give him a call."

Herb's cell went into voicemail and Gill left him a message to call and let him know what was holding him up. They waited another hour. I was getting worried. *Had he been arrested? Where is he?* "I'm calling his home and see if he's there."

"Oh my God. I am so sorry! Is there anything you need? Gill's here with me. I'll tell him. Are you sure we can't help? Please let us know. Bye. Again, I am so sorry."

When I ended the call I could tell immediately that Gill already knew what I was about to tell him. "Herb's gone. He died of an apparent heart attack. He was laying on the floor playing with his little grandson. It happened pretty sudden. His daughter walked into the family room to see how her dad was doing with her son. I guess she's in pretty bad shape. They sedated her and took her to the hospital for observation. I can't believe he's really gone."

By this time Gill had slumped into our booth and wept like a baby. Our server, who we had known for a long time came to our booth. Knowing something was really wrong seeing both of us a real mess she began weeping without even knowing what had happened. We told her and she went immediately to Eddy, the owner/manager. He turned the music off and got on the overhead speaker system. He announced that one of his best friends and customer had just passed away. "Herb was not only a good friend and customer but one of the best firefighters this city has ever had." And then there was complete silence. I had never heard it so quiet in The Hideout. Then Eddie asked that everyone finish their drink and then the Hideout would be dark until after Herb's funeral. Gill and I were really touched by this gesture.

Herb's funeral was the biggest ever held in our city. Family, friends, firefighters from as far away as just outside Chicago.

Gill and I met the Saturday after Herb's funeral. People were still talking about the friend they had lost. If only they knew what he had been doing for the past few years. It was good that they didn't know. He was a good husband, father, grandfather and friend. We will really miss him. The entire evening was spent talking about all the fun we had in school, summer vacations and the spring and winter breaks. Gill and I had a great time. We decided that we could continue to meet, if for no other reason, to honor our late friend.

We continued to meet for a few months. One Saturday evening Gill broke the bad news – he had terminal cancer. As a physician he fully understood the seriousness of his situation. I couldn't contain my sorrow, anger and other emotions. "Come on Gill, you can't just give up! We'll go to Mayo Clinic, anywhere you want to go. We can beat this thing. Please fight this man!"

Gill, with tears welling up in his eyes looked me straight in the face "Mark, don't you think I haven't explored every avenue, read every medical journal, called specialists around the country. I have an in-operable mass in my head. Those times that I told you and Herb and sometimes my wife, that I was going to a medical seminar, etc. Well, in actuality I was traveling the country trying to find answers. All to no avail. It's almost my time. I'm ready. Even though I haven't confessed to the police the crimes I've committed I still feel justified in my actions. Other than several doctors including the partners in our practice, you're the first to know. My family doesn't know.

"You gotta tell them Gill. Don't just pass away like Herb did. Give your family and friends some time to accept it. You owe them that much. Give them an opportunity to say their good-byes now."

Even though Gill said he would tell them I somehow felt that he never would. When I got home that evening I told Carol. Gill never swore me to secrecy. I wasn't going to tell his family but I felt that my wife had a right to know. She encouraged me to tell his family but I couldn't do it.

We met the next week at the Hideout. Gill couldn't drink any alcohol due to the strong chemo that he was on. "Gill you really look sick. Isn't someone in your family suspicious of your sudden weight loss? And look at your hair, that is, what you have left." He said that he thought his oldest son was beginning to suspect something was wrong.

Whether anyone suspected I'll probably never know. Before we departed company I felt compelled to ask him about his 'project'. I wondered if he was going to leave someone to carry on his quest. He said he wasn't sure but was pretty sure that one person would carry on. I begged him not to let me know who that person was. He said that who would take over the 'project' would be determined sometime on Monday. He said he would discuss things with his family Sunday afternoon.

As far as I know, Gill didn't have a chance to tell his family about his impending death and what he and Herb had been involved in. I don't think he had the opportunity to make sure someone was in place to carry on with what had become his passion. Gill was found dead in his bed Sunday morning. Less than 12 hours after we said good-bye. Little did I know that would be the last time I would see my friend.

Gill's funeral was not quite the same as Herb's but it was nice. A lot of people from the medical community attended. Since Gill was a physician and I might add, a very good one, he was somewhat obligated to join several clubs. He was a member of the country club for one. A lot of people in key positions in and around the city are members as well. A number of these 'key people' attended even though they really didn't know Gill. One of those attending was the Deputy Mayor. Another was the Chief of Police. I couldn't help but smile, almost laugh at the irony.

Now that my two best friends are gone I wondered if there would be more 'incidents'. It turned out that there were. I stayed away from the Hideout on Saturdays. For the most part, I ignored the reports on TV as well as the newspaper. I quit taking the evening paper and spent very little time reading the morning newspaper.

Three months passed by after Gill's death I still didn't know and didn't want to know who had stepped into Gill's and/Herb's shoes. The MO's regarding the incidents seemed to be just like they were before. The warnings from the police continued. These were warnings to anyone involved or having knowledge of violence, domestic or otherwise, to watch their back. They were encouraged to come forth with any information that might help them solve these crimes. I felt that to some extent the warnings could be directed to someone like me. I have a lot of information. But how and to whom do I report it?

End of Chapter Twelve

CHAPTER THIRTEEN

Police "Contacted"

The meetings with the three police teams – Homicide, Missing Persons, and Arson continued. They felt they were confident regarding who the 'recipients' were. The big questions were who and how were these things being carried out.

There are certain advantages to having my office in the same building as the police and courts. I was able to learn that these 'meetings of the minds' had continued. They were beginning to put things together finally. Maybe this is a good time to make contact with the initial investigating team (Jack & Maggie) to tell them that I have a 'theory.' I took extra measures to make sure that I didn't become a suspect. I used my experience with foster parenting as one of the reasons for my theory. I strongly suggested that they (the police) continue to put out a public warning to anyone involved in violence, domestic violence in particular. There **is** someone out there who might make them pay.

I communicated this via a fake email account sent from an internet café. I immediately deleted the account as soon as the email was sent. I told them that someone was hired to carry out the 'hits' but someone with a slightly higher IQ was arranging the 'hits'.

In the evening TV news and the morning newspaper the next day it was reported that the police had received an anonymous tip that may lead to an arrest soon. No other details were given.

The next week the police arrested a couple. Someone overheard them talking, of all places, at the Hideout. They were talking how disgusted they were regarding the incidence of domestic violence. It seemed to be just as bad as it was before the warnings that the police had issued. Warnings to anyone who might be thinking about hurting someone else. It doesn't seem like such a good idea to hurt other people living under the same roof as they. One of them stated that he knew what he would do to someone if he could get his hands on them.

This was enough to make them suspects. But it turned out that they alibied out for every single date and time someone was beaten, drugged or killed. They cut them loose but decided to put a tail on them for the next 72 hours or so.

End of Chapter Thirteen

CHAPTER FOURTEEN

It had been close to six months since losing Gill. I didn't feel very good about possibly tarnishing his or Herb's memory or reputation. I'm not sure why but I sent another email. Without mentioning their names I essentially told the whole story. They had already solved the missing librarian and the torching of the abandoned houses along with who beat the crap out of half the high school football team.

The houses were torched by a bunch of kids in the neighborhood. They said they did it just to watch the fire trucks come. To them, it was fun to watch the firefighters put out the fire.

The football players had their asses kicked by a group of guys who had taken the 'No More Bullying Pledge.'

As for Johnny, it turned out he **was** just like his father. He had grown tired of his 'boring life' and moved to Chicago. Probably so he could carry out his 'hobby' with less chance of being caught. He was sadly mistaking. He was extradited back to Indiana to face multiple charges including possession of child pornography.

When I sent the email I was careful to let them know that I didn't know anything until after the murders were committed. My two friends never intentionally caused anyone's death.

I made a huge mistake in sending the email. I forgot to delete the user account. It didn't take the police long to link it to me since I had been seen inside the café the same day and time the email was sent. My fingerprints and DNA were all over the computer used to send the email. My fingerprints were on file as a result of my being a lawyer.

I was sitting on my pool deck when the two detectives came out through the sliding glass doors that lead from our family room to the deck.

They had come to the front door asking for me. Carol had let them come in and lead them to the deck.

They each introduced themselves and asked me to do the same. Then they told me to put my hands behind my back. Before they could cuff me I begged them not to take me in handcuffs. My family didn't deserve to be subjected to the embarrassment of having the entire neighborhood watch as I was put into the back seat of a police vehicle in handcuffs. They read the Miranda rights while we were standing beside our pool. They walked me to their waiting police car. Carol's screams could be heard throughout the neighborhood. "Mark, what have you done? Why are you being arrested?" So much for trying to go quietly.

At the police station Jack and Maggie took turns questioning me. I asked "am I really under arrest? If so, I'm not going to say another word until my lawyer gets here." Even though I'm a lawyer I wasn't crazy enough to try to defend my own case. I called a good friend that I had met in law school. Jason Sanders. "Jason, this is Mark. Hey, I've got a bit of a problem. I'm being detained regarding an obstruction of justice and a few other related charges. Could you come down for my arraignment? I have plenty of assets to cover bail. Great, I'll see you then." I hung up the phone and turned to the detectives. "He's on his way. Could someone call my wife and let her know I'm ok?" Maggie handed the phone back to me. "Call your wife. I assume she doesn't know anything about what's been going on?" I looked back at her as I took the phone. "That was pretty slick, trying to get me to confess before my lawyer arrives and I really hope he gets here pretty soon. And, to answer your question, however, she doesn't know everything because I don't even know what I'm here for. Other than what you said at my house about being arrested for obstructing justice I'm in the dark here. Can I get a Diet Pepsi?"

I called Carol but she refused to talk to me. Except to call me a few choice words. Words I had never heard her use in speaking to me.

I sat quietly drinking my warm Diet Pepsi. Jason didn't arrive for another hour. "Jason, thanks for coming. Is there somewhere we can go where we can talk in private?"

Jason and I were lead to a room void of windows, mirrors or listening devices. There was a rather large table with chairs on either side. Jason removed pencil, paper and a small digital recorder from his brief case.

"Okay Mark, I'm looking at the charges and I gotta tell you this will not be an easy case to win. They've charged you with obstructing justice, assisting in multiple homicides, conspiracy to commit assault and battery, attempted murder, kidnapping. And that's just the major ones. Man, how could you have dug such a deep hole? I'm going to be representing you and I find it difficult to believe you are completely innocent. So let's start from the beginning. Just so you know, I'm recording this session. In addition, I'll be taking copious notes as we go. I'm all set up so why don't you start. I'll only stop you if I need clarification. Okay, let's do this."

With the recording picking up every word I was saying and with Jason writing most of it down I began. For clarification, I felt it necessary to go all the way back to the relationship Gill, Herb and I had. I covered my experience with the foster care days. I wanted to make sure that Jason and the court would understand that I knew nothing for sure during the early days of the case. To my knowledge, no homicides had occurred after I became aware of what was taking place. The other thing I wanted everyone to know was that I had absolutely no idea who took over things after my two best friends passed away. Jason tried not to interrupt me more than was absolutely necessary. I wanted everyone to know that I had never witnessed anything. I was going by what my friends had told me. The whole process took over three hours. By that time I was getting hungry and very tired.

Jason told me "I have all that I need for now Mark. I'll see you early in the morning for your arraignment hearing. I'm sorry you have to spend the night in jail. I'm confident that we'll be able to get you released after posting bail in the morning. We'll move forward from there. I need to go home and study through what you've given me. I need to plan a defense. It won't be easy."

I spent the night in jail. The next day I was taken to court for the hearing. Jason did the best he could considering the number of charges against me. He convinced the court that I was not a flight risk and should be released after posting bail. The bail was set at $100,000. I called my bank and arranged for $10,000 to be electronically transferred to the court. After what seemed like an eternity, I was released. Just for good measure they took my passport and placed a very stylish ankle bracelet on my left ankle. I was to stay in my home. If I had to leave for any reason they gave me a number to call. I was instructed to call the number and let them know where I was going. I was restricted to my home, my yard and the courthouse.

Jason drove me home. "I'll see you at my office in the morning. Let's plan on 10:30 and if needed we can continue talking over lunch. Get some rest. See you in the morning."

Carol didn't want me to enter the house but allowed me to come in to get some things. I packed a bag with enough clothes to last a few days. I tried to tell her what was going on but she refused to listen to me. I called my sister Mary to see if I could crash at her place for a few days. She and her husband live in an upscale, gated community about twenty minutes from my house. She had seen on the news that I had been arrested and charged with being involved in the murders, etc. that had taken place over the past few years. She was a little reluctant at first. It was her husband who convinced her to give me a chance to explain. I told her I would be there in about thirty minutes. After getting Mary's permission to stay at her house I called the number that I was instructed to call. I called to give them Mary's address but they told me I couldn't leave until a policeman arrived to take me there. Mary's address would be entered into the 'system' in place of my home address. I called Mary back and said I would call her as soon as my 'ride' arrived. When I got to her house I sat down with Mary and my brother-in-law, Bob to go over the whole thing. They both agreed that they would do the same for their best friends. It was comforting to know that someone in my family still believed in me.

The trial date was set for September 1st, just two months until I will have to account for being a friend. I had hoped to stay with my sister for a few days, a week tops, and by then I would have convinced Carol to let me come back home. It turned out that I would be staying at my sisters through the trial. It would be a long time before I would see my home again.

For the next two months I continued to meet with Jason in planning for the trial. During that time I spoke with each of my children on the phone. They didn't want to upset their mother by coming to see me. Carol wouldn't give me the time of day.

I began to grow weary of Jason's questions regarding exactly when I became aware of what my two best friends were doing. Jason told me to get used to it. He said in the court I would be asked these same questions over and over. I just wanted the whole thing to be **over**. Jason told me that he was pretty sure that I would be found guilty of at least some of the charges. He was going to try his best to minimize the damage. In other words, he would try to get me the minimum sentence. He began preparing me for the inevitable – I was likely going to prison. The question now is for how long.

As the trial date came closer and closer my emotions were all over the map. I would go from anger to hurt to feeling lonesome. I was really upset that my two best friends left me to face the charges they should have faced.

I was also concerned that during the trial it would be revealed who had committed the atrocities. Herb's and Gill's reputation would be dragged through the mud over and over. I was sure that Herb's and Gill's families would hate me.

I had hit the very bottom and couldn't see any chance for another moment of happiness or peace for the rest of my life.

Jason assured me that I had to be completely honest. I had to tell the court everything that I knew. I planned to do so in a way that would not make my two best friends sound like crazed criminals. It wasn't going to be easy.

Much to my surprise Carol and my children were seated in the gallery. With the exception of three phone calls from my three children I hadn't seen or heard from any of them since I left to live with my sister after Carol refused to let me back into my home. I looked their way but none of them made eye contact. However, they didn't turn away from me. They looked straight ahead as though they were in a trance. They weren't the only ones who felt that way. I felt like this whole thing was a dream. It was surreal.

The court was called to order and the charges were read. It seemed as though I was in a tunnel and the court official was just outside the tunnel. Jason had warned me that the D.A. was preparing to 'throw the book at me', but to hear the charges read so that everyone in the courtroom could hear was overwhelming. I folded my arms and placed them on the table. I rested my head on my arms thinking I could sleep and when I woke up it would be over. But such was not the case. Twice, the judge struck the gavel and ordered me to pay attention.

"The State of Indiana versus Mark Gibson......". *Wait a minute, that's me. I'm Mark. Who is 'the State'? Everybody in Indiana? My God, what have I done?*

The case against me was going to be difficult, if not impossible, to defend. Jason had met with the judge and the D.A. prior to the trial. They all agreed that neither Herb nor Gill would be mentioned by name. The charges were against me. I knew who the perpetrators were but refused to give them up until after their passing. In the opening arguments the court would be told that all who were involved had since deceased. The two 'goons' however were identified and the court was told about their involvement and that they had since died in a police chase. Who had hired them could not be proven. The names given to the police were names of deceased persons. Their involvement was all hearsay.

The charges - conspiracy to commit murder – 11 counts, conspiracy to commit assault, kidnapping, sodomy, breaking and entering. I thought the guy reading the charges would never stop. I thought to myself, if that was someone other than me I would be ready to lock them up forever. But it **is** me they were talking about.

After the charges had been read the trial began. The A.D.A. representing the state gave her opening statement. Then Jason gave his. He argued that none of these charges were legitimate. I was merely an innocent by-stander. I had never witnessed any of the 'crimes' and I had never participated in any way. As for the murder charges, I didn't even know about my friends' involvement until after the murders, rape and sodomy had occurred. The guys that did it were dead.

The trial went on for just over two weeks. The State called several witnesses including the detectives that had investigated the cases. The two 'primary' witnesses were detectives Jack Carlson and Maggie Donaldson, who by now were Mr. & Mrs. Carlson. They, along with the other detectives and law enforcement personnel could only speak to what they knew about how the victims were killed or injured and where they had been found. The only knowledge they had regarding me was what they saw in the emails that I sent. In none of them did I implicate myself. I only said that I had information regarding who had made the arrangements for who was to be 'taken care of' and where they might be found.

On Thursday, September 18th both sides gave their final summations and rested. It was now up to the jury to decide my fate.

I tried to talk with Carol and my kids but they left the courtroom before I had the opportunity to do so.

Jason and I went to the cafeteria in the lower level of the courthouse. We were hoping the jury wouldn't be out too long. After we had a light snack and several cups of coffee Jason suggested that we leave and get some rest. We would be contacted as soon as the jury had a verdict.

I spent the night at my sister's house where I paced the floor, sleep eluding me. Somewhere after 3 AM, I finally dosed off in a chair.

It was after 9 o'clock the next morning when I awakened. The combination of lack of sleep and spending about 6 hours sleeping in a chair took a toll on my body. I was stiff, my head ached as bad as it ever had and I felt like I wasn't going to survive another day. Then reality set in. *Holy crap, I have to return to the courthouse and wait for the jury to decide my fate.*

I called Jason to let him know I was awake and would be ready to go in about an hour. He told me to relax. The jury had retired for the night and hadn't even began deliberations. We planned to go to the courthouse in the afternoon.

Around 3 in the afternoon Jason called me. He said that the jury reported to the judge that they were deadlocked but agreed to continue deliberating. This was Friday. I thought if they were still deadlocked at the end of the day they may not have a verdict until Monday. However, Jason assured me that they had been sequestered and would continue deliberations through the weekend. Court would reconvene when the jury was ready. Even if it is Saturday or Sunday. That didn't happen. After a miserable weekend Jason and I returned to the courthouse on Monday morning. Mary was kind enough to go with me. At least one member of my family believed in my innocence. Mary is a nurse. She works three days a week, twelve hours a day. This happened to be one of her days off.

We spent most of the morning in the cafeteria. Jason suggested that my sister and I get out of the building and get some fresh air. He would take the responsibility of letting them know that I hadn't fled. But was just taking a walk.

In September the weather can be anywhere from warm to cold and raining. That day was absolutely perfect. We walked around the downtown mall window shopping like we did when we were kids. It was one of the nicest September afternoons I could remember. We both had our cell phones with us in the event that we would need to return to the courthouse. Jason called my cell around 4:30 to say that the jury decided to retire for the day. Since Jason had taken us downtown we decided to ride a bus home. Another thing we hadn't done since we were kids. Back then it cost a dime to ride and another two cents for a transfer. That day it cost us three bucks.

Jason made the call to let them know that the 'prisoner' was taking a bus home.

After another restless night I woke up at 7:40 feeling like I had not even been asleep. I shaved and got a quick shower. My sister had to work that day so I had the house to myself. I really felt lonely. I thought *if I go to prison, this is what it will be like.*

I didn't have to feel lonely very long. At 12:30 Jason called to tell me the jury was in and we needed to get to the courthouse **now**. I was going to drive but Jason reminded me that if I'm found guilty of any of the charges I may not be permitted to return home. He would pick me up in fifteen minutes.

It was just after 1PM when we arrived at the courthouse. We parked and walked as fast as we could to the courtroom.

The courtroom was nearly full. Carol and the kids were not there. I had called Mary to tell her that the jury was in. I didn't expect her to get away to come to the courthouse but she said she would call Bob and see if he could come. When I walked into the courtroom Bob was seated behind the defense side. He was just two rows behind me. That really made me feel good.

The court was called to order and the judge asked the jury foreman if the jury had reached a verdict. His answer "we have your honor." The judge asked "what is your verdict?" The foreman began to read a litany of charges and 'findings'. "As to the count of conspiracy to commit murder, we find the defendant innocent. As to the count of ...." The foreman continued to read the count followed by we find the defendant innocent. But then came the final charge "as to the charge of withholding information and obstruction of justice, we find the defendant guilty."

I looked over at Jason and he seemed to be pleased with the outcome but still looked a little concerned.

The judge asked the foreman "is this decision unanimous?" "It is your honor" was the reply.

It was over. But what does it mean? What's the punishment for obstructing justice and withholding information?

The judge asked for order and said "the defendant is released and must return to this courtroom at nine o'clock Monday, October 6th for sentencing." I had less than two weeks to get my affairs in order.

Jason met me outside the courtroom. "Are you ready to go back to Mary's house?"

As he drove to Mary's house we discussed the decision and what it could possibly mean. Jason said it could result in probation with community service to the maximum of twenty years in prison. He would make a plea for leniency but there were no guarantees. He said that we should plan for the worst and hope for the best.

Over the next couple weeks I tried, unsuccessfully to meet with Carol. She refused. My kids however, agreed to meet with me at Mary's house. They had seen on the news that I was found innocent of all but one charge. I explained to them that I was trying to be faithful to my best friends. Even though I knew what they were doing was wrong I didn't do enough to make them stop. If I was guilty of anything it was poor judgment. They said they believed me and would try to get their mother to understand. I wasn't so sure that would ever happen.

I met with my pastor and also with Michael j during this period. My pastor assured me that even though I was guilty before man that God would forgive me. He prayed with me and I feel that I have been forgiven. I had met Michael j about two years ago at a conference on, of all things, violence. We had coffee a few times after that. I asked him if he would be willing to write about my situation whether I went to prison or not. We discussed it in detail and he agreed to work something out.

The balance of the time before my sentencing was spent visiting many friends. I met with both Gill's and Herb's widows. Both of them said that they suspected something was going down. During the court proceedings they watched the news on one of the local television stations. Knowing about the close relationship that I had with Herb and Gill each of them deduced that at least one of them was involved. However both widows stated they had never discussed it. They both seemed to understand that I had no option in reporting the information to the police. I thanked them and said it was important to meet with them in case I went to prison. It might be awhile before we meet again. The thought of going to prison didn't bother me as much as thinking about my two best friends. They were no longer here to give me their support. I really miss them.

I just had the weekend to go before I faced the judge again. On Saturday I helped Bob with some of his autumn chores like raking leaves, clearing the garden and flower beds. We worked from early morning until darkness made it difficult to continue. I went to bed exhausted but feeling like I had accomplished something worthwhile. I only wished I had been doing the same work at my own house. On Sunday I went to church. I was hoping to see Carol there but she stayed away. I'm sure she knew that I would be there. She was not ready to confront the situation just yet. I knew it would take some time but I was sure that we would reconcile at some point.

I woke up Monday morning at about 6:30. I had plenty of time to shave, shower and eat a light breakfast. Thankfully, both Mary and Bob had arranged to be off work and could go with me. Jason and I had met Friday afternoon. He prepared me for the sentencing process. He told me that he had spoken with both the judge and D.A. He had made a plea with both of them to show leniency on me. However, he had a bad feeling about the judge. He also reminded me that I would have the opportunity to address the court. I was prepared. I had been working on it for quite some time.

I was surprised to see the courtroom filled when we arrived. Carol and the kids were there. My pastor, Michael j, several detectives and many of my friends and colleagues were there as well.

Once again, the court was called to order. Silence filled the courtroom. The judge was looking very stern when he began to speak. "Mr. Gibson, the offence of obstructing justice and withholding evidence is a very serious matter. Lives could have been saved, people could have been spared the harsh punishment perpetrated upon them by a kangaroo court. But only if you had seen fit to speak up and put a stop to these atrocities. You didn't, and now you must pay the price. Before I pronounce his sentence the defendant may address the court."

I began by telling them that I only had my suspicions for the first several months that these 'atrocities' had taken place. I posed the question "what would you do if you were put into that situation?" As I asked that question I first looked at the judge and then turned to face everybody in the courtroom. Including my wife and family. I continued by giving them details of my meetings with my friends. I reminded them that ALL directly involved are now deceased. If anyone is attacked or murdered I don't know who they are. My last statement was an apology to my family, friends, the police and the court. At that point I once again took my seat next to Jason.

There was, once again, silence in the courtroom. I felt as though I was transported to another place in time and space. As the judge read the sentence it was as though I managed to escape the courtroom and was listening to someone speak from afar.

"Withholding information and obstructing justice is a very serious crime. Because of your reluctance to come forward lives were lost and people were subjected to a litany of offences. You told this court that you were protecting your friends. I believe that's true. However, it's my opinion that you were protecting your own reputation, your license to practice law and embarrassment to your family. As judge of the court I am bound to impose a penalty on you Mr. Gibson. The punishment for this particular offence can be anywhere from probation to twenty years in prison. Probation would not be appropriate in this case. Twenty years is a little harsh. Therefore, I am sentencing you to ten years with the possibility of parole after serving five years and good behavior. Good luck to you Mr. Gibson. Please take Mr. Gibson to holding pending transfer to Shadeland Correctional Facility. This court is adjourned."

I was placed in handcuffs.

I looked first at my family. They were all crying. Mary and Bob were in tears. Jason was really upset. I couldn't help but hear the judge's words as they echoed in my head – "it is my opinion that you were protecting your own…….."

I thought *what a crock. It was **always** about my two best friends.*

Jason told me that he would visit with me prior to my being taken to prison. I asked him if he could arrange a visit with my wife and family. He said he would work on it. He couldn't convince them so I didn't see any family members other than Mary and Bob. Two days later I was taken to prison to serve at least five years. That's five birthdays for Carol, my three kids, myself. Five Christmases…….

End of Chapter Fourteen

****

Misery and torture, both a part of me.

Suicide eventually will surely come to be.

The evil seed inside grows larger every day.

The voice inside my head now I must obey.

****

CHAPTER FIFTEEN

Prison Life

The moment I stepped off the prison bus I felt sub-human. More like an animal. It is the absolute worst feeling ever. *The* 'intake process' brings you down even further. Undressing in front of strangers being poked and prodded. Having every cavity in your body searched, taking a shower in front of others really adds to the embarrassment. Then there's the prison garb and watching them take your clothes away... WOW! *Do I really deserve this?*

Even though Jason had petitioned the court to not place me amongst the regular prison population it was not granted. Fortunately, I got a pretty good cell-mate. He had only been in for a couple of months. Long enough to know his way around and to be in a position to walk me through the 'system'. To this day, I really appreciate Ralph.

Today, I begin day number one of what could possibly be 1800+ days. I decided not to attempt to count the days.

It only took me about a week to become familiar with the 'rules' and to learn that there are two sets of rules. One is the rules of the prison itself. The much harsher set of rules are those handed down by a certain group of inmates. I decided to follow ALL of the rules but that I would not compromise my beliefs. Nor would I be anybody's 'bitch' etc. I only got into two fights but when the prison officials weighed the evidence I received no punishment. I never had one day added to my sentence. One night I began to pray 'Lord, I've been in worse situations….. But then I realized that NO I have NEVER been in anything as bad as this, much less anything remotely worse.

My children began visiting me after six weeks, six really long weeks. It took Carol three months before she agreed to visit. As he promised, Jason visited me as soon as 'they' would allow it. My pastor did the same.

It was still very, very lonely. I learned very quickly that I needed to choose very carefully who I would let into my little world. It turned out that there were only two that I really became friends with. Although slightly different, it was like the old days of the 'gang of three'.

End of Chapter Fifteen

CHAPTER SIXTEEN

Being in prison has to be the most humiliating experiences a person can suffer.

Even though I enjoy my visits from Michael and the visits from Carol I detest the strip search after each visit. What could I possibly be smuggling into this place?

As I stated in the previous chapter Carol didn't visit me for the first several months of my incarceration. Those were the most miserable months of my entire life. We were not together for Christmas for the first time in our marriage. She was disappointed and ashamed of what I had gotten myself into. Over time she finally found it in her heart to forgive me. This is due in no small part to Michael, our pastor and God Himself. Michael and I could probably write another book just about that.

Carol visits me every other week and Michael visits me on alternate weeks. I have a visitor every week. Our pastor usually comes with Carol. But sometimes, he feels it best to give my wife and me some 'alone time'. That's really laughable. Nobody gets any 'alone time' in this place. We visit in a large open room with tables (similar to picnic tables) and chairs. I am told where to sit and then once I am seated my visitors can join me.

At no time during the visit am I allowed to leave my seat. At the end of the visit (maximum of one hour) I have to stay in my seat until my visitor(s) leave the room and then I can go and get strip searched before I return to my 'room'.

My children visited at first but then found it too difficult (emotionally) so they have stopped. I really miss my kids. As for my grandchildren, I can't even begin to describe how much I miss them. The youngest is six months old. She'll be ready to start elementary school by the time I see her. I am hoping (and praying) to reconcile with them once I am home. Both

Michael and my pastor have agreed to participate in the reconciliation process. We'll see how it goes.

I would like to write another book after I am released but I'm not sure. I only have a few more months before being released. I should be home just in time for Christmas. My first in a very long time. It's been over four years since I've had the privilege of sleeping in my own bed and possibly getting to sleep with Carol. Although, she and I haven't discussed that yet. We'll see….

End of Chapter Sixteen

FINAL THOUGHT

If you are involved, in any way whatsoever, with violence of any kind, just know this – there are plenty of people like Herb and Gill out there. Just watching and waiting on the law to take action. They're pissed, sick and tired of too many people refusing to take some sort of action. When the law doesn't take action someone else just might.

The End

SPECIAL ACKNOWLEDGEMENTS

Poems following some of the chapters in this book were written by one of my Foster Daughters. You can see and feel her pain through the words of each poem. With her permission I share these with you. Many years later she has yet to heal completely from the Terror in the Night. On the next page is one of my favorites.

****

Caresses like knives sting my flesh,
I hide within the pain.
I pray for help, it never comes.
Nothing will ever change.

I feel his breath upon my skin,
It makes me cringe inside.
He talks to me, whispers my name.
He never sees me cry

He doesn't know where I go.
He never sees my face.
He doesn't know that I'm not there.
Someone else has taken my place.

****

"Thanks Tasha, I love you very much."

Dad

EPILOGUE

Prior to writing this book I made the decision to learn more about the subject of violence. I don't consider myself as a pacifist. The whole idea and reason for violence totally escapes me. When I was growing up movies and TV contained a certain amount of violence but today it is extremely graphic. This, I believe has had an influence on the number of violent acts committed in our society today. I started cutting out articles from the newspaper. I paid a little closer attention to TV and radio news. Then finally, I sat down at my computer, went on-line and began searching the topic of violence. Much of the following is a result of my "research".

DISCUSSION ON VIOLENCE

Violence – A global issue:

According to the **World Health Organization:** *"Globally, violence takes the lives of more than 1.5 million people annually. Just over 50% due to suicide, some 35% due to homicide, and just over 12% as a direct result of war or some other form of conflict. For each single death due to violence, there are dozens of hospitalizations, hundreds of emergency department visits, and thousands of doctors' appointments. Furthermore, violence often has lifelong consequences for victims' physical and mental health and social functioning and can slow economic and social development."*

Sadly, violence **is** preventable. Evidence shows strong relationships between levels of violence and potentially modifiable factors such as concentrated poverty, income and gender inequality, the harmful use of alcohol, and the absence of safe, stable and nurturing relationships between children and parents. Scientific research shows that strategies addressing the underlying causes of violence can be effective in preventing violence. Examples of scientifically credible strategies to forestall violence embody nurse home-visiting and parenting education to prevent child maltreatment; life skills coaching for children ages 6-18 years; school-based programs to handle gender norms and attitudes; reducing alcohol handiness and misuse through enactment and social control of liquor licensing laws, taxation and pricing; reducing access to guns knives; and promoting gender equality by, to illustrate, supporting the economic authorization of women.

Violence is outlined by the World Health Organization as *"the intentional use of physical force or power, vulnerable or actual, against oneself, another person, or against a gaggle or community that either ends up in or has a high probability leading to injury, death, psychological hurt, organic process deficits or deprivation. The inclusion of the word "power," additionally to the phrase "use of physical force," broadens the character of a violent act and expands the standard understanding of violence to incorporate those acts that result from an influence relationship, as well as threats and intimidation. The "use of power" conjointly serves to incorporate neglect or acts of omission, in addition to the more obvious violent acts of commission. Thus, "the use of physical force or power" ought to be understood to incorporate neglect and every kind of physical, sexual and psychological abuse, as well as suicide and other self-abusive acts. This definition intentionality associates with the committing of the act itself, regardless of the end result it produces."*

Most of us, myself included, and maybe you, the reader have seen this first-hand. The act itself is dangerous enough however the continuing, typically womb-to-tomb, effects are often devastating. Not only to the victim but to his/her family, friends, co-workers, neighbors. Almost anyone with whom she/he comes into contact is affected.

In my on-line search I discovered that there are many kinds of violence. I actually have listed them here:

Self-directed violence – self-destructive behavior

Interpersonal violence – family and/or intimate partner violence

Collective violence – social, political and economic violence

Once again, from the World Health Organization: *"Violence in altogether accounts for over 1.5 million deaths a year, some 90% occur in low-middle income countries – 52% due to suicide, 33.5% due to homicide, and just over 12% due to wars."* This indicates the magnitude of violence.

Continuing my research, I discovered that the kind of violence can be a result of the *nature* of the violent act. They are listed below.

Physical abuse

Sexual abuse

Psychological abuse

Abuse involving deprivation or neglect

I conjointly found that there exists several <u>causes of violence</u>. They are:

<u>Biological </u>and <u>private factors</u> that influence how individuals behave and increase their probability of turning into either a **victim** or **perpetrator** of violence: demographic characteristics (age, education, income),

temperament disorders, substance abuse, and a history of experiencing, witnessing or engaging in violent behavior at some point in their lives.

Close relationships, such as those with family and friends. In **youth violence** having friends who engage in or encourage violence can increase a young person's risk of being a victim or perpetrator of violence. For **intimate partner** violence a uniform marker is marital conflict or discord in the relationship. In **elder abuse**, necessary factors are stress due to the nature of the past relationship between the abused person and the care giver.

Community context – schools, workplaces and neighborhoods. Risk could also be affected by factors such as the existence of a **neighborhood drug trade**, the **absence of social networks** and focused financial **poverty**. All of these factors have shown to be necessary in many kinds of violence.

Broad societal factors help to facilitate a climate in which violence is inspired or pent-up. This might be due to the responsiveness of the **criminal justice system**, **social and cultural norms** regarding gender roles or **parent-child relationships**, **income inequality**, the strength of the **social welfare system**, the social **acceptability of violence**, the availability of **firearms**, the **exposure** to violence in **mass media**, and **political instability.**

Social media, such as Facebook has been an enormous cause for perpetrating violence. I'm not essentially blaming Facebook. However, it is a **tool** that may, and is, accustomed to trigger anger very quickly. A decade or so ago if you had a "bone to pick" with somebody you'd sometimes write them a note, call them on the phone, or simply "put the word out" that you were prepared for a fight. Or typically you could simply begin a nasty rumor just to piss them off. With Facebook, Twitter, etc. someone will misuse social media by putting something out there that is extremely hurtful and harmful to another person's reputation. It goes out to a **very large community of "viewers"** and might **stay** out there for long periods of time. The "victim" will solely refute the negative comments in hopes that folks will choose to believe him/her rather than the original "author."

The following is a true story. It was reported in the Indianapolis Star Newspaper and on local TV.

A few years ago, in Indianapolis, somebody put some very negative comments about another person on Twitter and Facebook. The "target" took offence and challenged the "author" to a fight (kind of like 'Gunfight at the OK Corral.') There were two groups – all females between the ages of 20 and 22. They chose to call themselves 'groups', not 'gangs.' *I guess 'group' sounds more 'ladylike.'* The two groups, via Facebook decided on a time and place to meet and 'settle this thing.' As far as the police know, none of the 'ladies' were packing heat. Problem is their boyfriends showed up and at least some of them **were** armed. Several boyfriends of the group that appeared to be losing the battle arrived at the scene. At about the same time boyfriends of the other group arrived. They began firing their weapons at the opposing group. The other side returned fire. When it was all over five females and two males were wounded. The boyfriend of one of the young females tried to make a get-away. Later, police found the body of a 22 year old in the backseat of his car. She was a State Girls High School Basketball All Star and member of a state university basketball team. She was in college on a full scholarship for basketball. She was dead in the back seat. The driver of the car was caught a short distance away with a gunshot wound to his leg, his young girlfriend dead in the backseat. What a shame! What an absolute waste of human life!

Using the information that I have given you thus far, I would say that this is a classic case of **interpersonal violence** (type) of a **psychological nature** (nature) caused by **Community/Broad Societal** factors (cause).

Unless you've been living in a cave in some far off place or you've been asleep or in a coma for the past several decades, you've read many newspaper accounts and have heard many radio/TV reports regarding violence. Violence seems to be everywhere - on our streets and in our homes. Unfortunately, it occurs every second of every day. However, there is one type of violence that I will <u>never</u> understand. That is <u>domestic violence</u>. It is a huge problem throughout the world. I am genuinely concerned about the problem in America.

Unfortunately, it doesn't look as though it has gotten any better over the last few decades. Unless we take some action against it, violence of every kind will likely continue to get worse.

Think about this: What other species on planet Earth do you know of where there is as much violence within the confines of the "home?" In the 'animal kingdom' the dominant male often attacks his offspring and/ or his mate for no apparent reason. But we're talking about animals far down the chain of existence. Wild animals and in some cases domesticated animals attack each other. But often this is a result of poor training or poor care. We've all seen it happen with domesticated animals (such as dogs). Many of these animals are trained to fight and even kill. In the wilderness undomesticated animals hunt their prey, attack and then usually devour. This is a matter of hunger, survival or just the natural order of things.

Humans, for many reasons, both unknown and known, are supposed to be different from other forms of life. But very often the human species is no different than lower life forms. For example, the husband or boyfriend who feels obligated to show that he is without fear and displays it by beating his wife or girlfriend and in many cases his children or the children of his girlfriend. Why? Is it because of drugs or alcohol? Drugs and/or alcohol certainly contribute in large part to the problem. But, not always. What makes a person attack an innocent child and force him or her to participate (unwillingly) in sordid sexual acts? When we think of violence, particularly, domestic violence, we think of men as being the perpetrators. Not always. It's not uncommon for a mother to allow or even encourage her boyfriend(s) to abuse her children. Often times the mother is a participant and in some cases she acts alone.

Check today's edition of your local newspaper. How many acts of violence do you see? What about the local or national news today? If you live in or near a medium to large metropolitan area, as I do, then I would be shocked if you didn't find a few articles depicting violence or the threat thereof.

Even though I have spent some time defining and discussing Violence in general, most of this book addresses the issue of Domestic Violence. To me, one of the lowest forms of domestic violence is sexual abuse. This type often is never reported or if reported the perpetrator is never punished. No proof. He said/she said and on and on it goes….

Domestic violence often claims a child as its victim. Typically the perpetrator is a step-father, boyfriend, neighbor or even a family member. Primarily, young girls are the victims but it is not unusual for the victim to be a young boy. The perpetrator could be either male or female. Typically the motive is driven by deviate sexual behavior.

To a child or to <u>anyone</u> being awakened in the night to feel an unwelcomed hand touching places that are very private to you, places that

<u>nobody</u> should ever touch or see can and does reign down TERROR on the 'victim'. As a child, you're not really sure why those places shouldn't be 'invaded' but you know that they are your private places. Later in 'the visit' you are told that you **must** touch places on this **monster**. Places that should be private to him/her. So why is he making you do this? "What is wrong with <u>me</u>?" you ask yourself. "I must be really bad if I am doing this." When he/she is finished he/she leaves. Leaving you alone in the dark to think about what had just happened. Leaving you alone in the dark to feel dirty. To feel guilty of participating in this terrible exercise. And then you cry yourself to sleep only to awaken in the morning to wonder when the **monster** will visit next. After all, he lives here. He's your Mother's boyfriend.

As the years go by the victim is left with this guilt and shame. He or she is often left with the nightmares of the **monster's visits**. It's very possible that nothing was ever done about these 'assaults' as the victim later learns. Perhaps he or she tried to tell their mother only to have her say that it must be your imagination. He (her boyfriend, the **monster**) is really a good guy and that she loves him very much. When you're old enough you move out and on your own. Carrying the nightmares with you.

What was just described happens every day in homes throughout our country and in many parts of the world. It's called sexual abuse, child abuse, assault. All of which are crimes punishable by prison terms. Too many times however, there is no arrest, there is no trial, and there is no punishment. Not for **the monster**, that is. But for the young girl or boy who was the victim life will never be normal. Fear takes up residence inside this innocent victim and likely will never leave. As a former foster parent, I know this to be true. I've witnessed it first-hand.

FROM THE AUTHOR

All characters depicted in this book are fictional. Any resemblance between someone you may know and the characters in the book are purely coincidental. Even though this is a book of fiction, it is my desire that you have enjoyed reading this story and will gain a better understanding of the problem we (all humans on planet earth) face. I would encourage you to study the subject in greater detail. You might want to begin by simply going to the internet and Google – *violence* or *domestic violence*. You will be amazed at the amount of information that is at your fingertips. All within a few key strokes.

After you have a better understanding of the problem TAKE SOME ACTION!

I'm not suggesting that you take the law into your own hands as Herb and Gill did. But you can ....

Thank you,
Michael j

Printed in the United States
By Bookmasters